BOOK
TWO
GUARDING HER HEART

Never Admire an Adventurer

REGINA SCOTT

*To my own adventurers, whose progress I applaud
and delight in, and to the Lord, who offers us
adventure beyond our dreams.*

CHAPTER ONE

Near Weyton, Surrey, England
November 1825

HOW SURPRISING THAT rebellion could feel so satisfying.

Julia Hewett had been fighting with her temper as long as she could remember. Her mother had liked to tease that a fiery red head meant a fiery heart. Generally, she did her best to get along. But her father had gone too far this time.

She settled herself on the saddle, gaze sweeping the road that passed their estate. Drops from the recent rain sparkled on the lawns running down from the house, making the grass look as if it were made of emeralds in the cool autumn air. A raven headed for the row of trees in the distance, black against the grey of the sky.

Any moment, her bodyguard would come riding in. Father had said it would be today, and Father was rarely wrong. That was one of the reasons he'd managed to amass a fortune great enough to buy this country estate two hours west of London. His supreme self-reliance was also why he didn't entirely trust anyone else's opinions.

Even hers.

Edevane pawed the ground, head bobbing. The stallion could likely think of better ways to spend his time than to wait upon her good pleasure.

Julia patted the sleek black neck. "Just a few more moments, my sweet. I'll be in a great deal of trouble if Father speaks to Mr. Tanner before I do."

She still couldn't believe her father had hired Kristof Tanner to act as her bodyguard. For one thing, he was a former member of the Batavarian Imperial Guard, used to protecting kings and princes, not daughters of entrepreneurs. For another, she hadn't seen anything approaching danger in all her three and twenty years. Her father's wealth and attention had all but guaranteed that. Yes, they'd heard reports of highwaymen in the area. And yes, her friend Abigail Winchester had nearly been kidnapped in the churchyard only last month, but that had had to do with secrets from her past.

Julia only had one secret. And he had just appeared on the horizon.

She wasn't sure how she knew it was him at that distance. The road was well traveled. Since she and Edevane had been waiting, three carriages and four men on horseback had passed. But none carried themselves with that easy confidence, as if daring the world to offer a rebuke.

Something fluttered inside her, like a moth seeking a flame. Very likely it came from the knowledge of what she must say to him.

He turned onto the drive to Hewett House and reined in beside her. "Miss Hewett. You didn't need to ride out to welcome me." His gaze went down the gravel drive toward the house. "And with no one to accompany you."

She had no intention of allowing her companion, Daring, much less one of the grooms to overhear this conversation.

"I am well within sight of the house, sir," she said. "And these are my father's lands. No one would harm me here."

"Very good news," he said with a nod. "My job should be easy, then."

"Very easy," she assured him, sizing up the gelding he rode. He must have borrowed it from Rose Hill, where he and his comrades were staying while their patroness, Lady Belfort, sought to find them positions in England now that their sovereign had returned home. "However, we must develop our strategy before you take up your position."

He cocked his head, revealing a bit of russet hair under his hat. "Strategy? I've been acting as bodyguard to King Frederick, the Crown Prince, and his courtiers for ten years. Do you think I need schooling?"

Heat was building in her cheeks. She ignored it. "No, of course not, though I don't doubt my father will have something to say about your responsibilities. I merely wanted to explain a few of my expectations."

He nodded toward the road. "Perhaps we can talk while we ride."

She turned Edevane, who settled in beside the gelding with a shake of his dark head. "Thank you. I understand it will be your duty to protect me whenever we leave the estate."

"Whenever you leave the house," he corrected her. "And when company calls as well."

Her father had been stricter than she'd thought. "I pity you. My life isn't that interesting."

He flashed her a smile. "Oh, I'm sure we can contrive."

Gooseflesh skittered along her arms under her wool riding habit. This, more than anything, was why she'd known she must speak to him. Kristof Tanner was a potent force on the best of days. She must not allow that attraction to pull her off course.

"Exactly," she said. "Father will likely speak to you, if he hasn't already, about which gentlemen I'm allowed to partner at dances and such. I may at times suggest a different choice."

His mouth quirked. "Ah. You have a suitor you favor."

"Yes," she said, pleased that he'd caught on so quickly. "Lord Westerbrook. But Father isn't too keen on him."

Tanner urged his horse up a slight rise in the drive. "Not rich enough?"

Edevane took the change in elevation easily. "Not titled enough," Julia explained with a grimace. "Father wants a duke. I want a man who will love and honor me all the days of his life. A man I can love and honor in return. The other details don't matter one whit."

Once more his mouth quirked, as if her declaration amused him, but she could not find it in her to take offense. She probably sounded impossibly idealistic prosing on about love and honor when a good number of marriages had neither, according to her father. He saw marriage as a bargain, something else he could negotiate, as he'd negotiated his way from pit boy in a coal mine to the owner of multiple enterprises. Given such a heritage and example, surely she could negotiate a better marriage for herself.

"Very well," he said as the house loomed closer. "I'm sure we can reach an agreement."

Already she could see grooms coming out of the stable block to see to her horse and his. Any moment, a footman would open the front door as well. Edevane resisted as she slowed his steps.

"More importantly," she said, drawing on every ounce of courage she possessed, "we must decide what to tell my father of our previous meetings, before we find ourselves engaged."

He had forgotten how pretty she was, how earnest. Under her short-crowned riding hat, her thick red hair was tamed back from a face with delicate features. Those big brown eyes fixed on him as if her life depended on his answer. Very likely that intensity was what had drawn him to her in the first place. That and the fact that he could never abide seeing a woman cry. He had been trained to be a hero, and heroes did not stand by when needed. He could imagine that any number of men, including this Lord Westerbrook, would be delighted to find themselves forced into an engagement.

But not him. He had plans for his future, and a wife could be an impediment.

So could this job. Bodyguard to an heiress. A shame it wasn't to her father. John Hewett, his patroness Lady Belfort had told him, traveled to more interesting places than shopping or the local assembly. Still, if Tanner did a good job, her father might be willing to recommend him to others who could give him the life of adventure he craved. That recommendation would not happen if Hewett thought Tanner had used his daughter badly.

"I take it you haven't told him, then," he said, slowing the gelding's pace as well. Lady Belfort had allowed him the use of the horse, saying that Julia could return him when next she came to visit. If Mr. Hewett's other horses were anything like the Thoroughbred next to him, he wouldn't mind sending this horse back in exchange.

"No," she admitted. "Please understand I will be forever in your debt. I was distraught that night you discovered me in the duke's garden. You sat, you listened, you showed compassion. It was exactly what I needed."

She made him sound a paragon. He shifted on the saddle. "It was only the duty of a gentleman to a lady in distress."

"Regardless," she said, "if my father knew you and I had met alone in a moonlit garden, I doubt he would have hired you as my bodyguard. I can only be glad he was in the card room when you and I encountered each other again at the last assembly."

He was just as glad. He had no excuse for seeking her

out the second time except that it had pleased him to dance with the prettiest girl in attendance. He hardly wanted her father to come calling, pistol in hand. That wouldn't help either of their reputations.

"I'll say nothing," he promised. "It will be our secret."

"Thank you." She breathed out the words moments before they arrived in the stable yard.

Tanner glanced around as he dismounted. Hewett House was well situated, with fields in all directions. They would certainly see any enemy coming. The stables had multiple stalls, mostly filled, and room for three carriages. He gave the reins to a tousled-haired lad, then turned to find one of the other grooms had already handed her down. He wasn't sure why that disappointed him. Likely just anticipating his job as her bodyguard.

He lifted down his satchel and sword, then fell into step beside her as she headed toward the house. It was square and solid, built of the buttery stone he was coming to equate with England. Urns as big as a man stood on either side of the entry stairs. Good cover, if he needed it.

A tall, silver-maned fellow in a black tailcoat opened the front door for them and let them into a marble-tiled entry hall with rosewood stairs curving up one side to the next story. "Miss Hewett." He raised an impeccable brow at the sight of Tanner beside her.

"Mr. Garrison," she said, "this is Mr. Tanner, the bodyguard Father hired for me. I believe you were expecting him."

The butler's nostrils flared, as if he'd smelled something unpleasant. Tanner returned the look from a good two inches higher. Garrison raised his chin as if to make up the difference.

"Indeed," he said. "This way."

Julia sent Tanner a commiserating look before starting up the stairs. The butler, however, led him down a corridor toward the back of the house.

Tanner quickly saw why. "The servant's stair?"

Garrison regarded him again. "Family and guests take the main stair. You are not family, and you are not a guest."

And that was where he stood in this household.

He had to turn sideways to keep his shoulders from brushing the walls as he followed the butler up the dimly lit stairs. They passed the first landing, and the second, until he wondered how many more floors could be above them. At last, Garrison came out into a corridor with multiple doors, closely spaced, opening off it. He nodded to the door across from them.

Tanner took two steps inside. The room didn't allow much more than that. It had blue walls, as if he had climbed high enough to reach the sky. He could tell at a glance that the bed wasn't long enough for him to stretch out. Besides its iron frame, a scratched bureau and washstand with a chipped pitcher were the only other furnishings. He wouldn't even have his own fire. The space was warm at the moment, but it likely would be freezing by morning. All in all, it was a far cry from the palaces in which he'd stayed for the last ten years.

"This won't do," he said, turning to the butler, who raised his brows again. "I need to be closer to Miss Hewett if I'm to protect her."

"If your protection is required," Garrison said, doubt lacing every syllable, "you will be called for."

"If you wait until the danger is here, calling for me may be too late," Tanner pointed out. "And where do you intend for me to store my short sword, knives, pistol, and lead."

Garrison drew himself up. "I am quite certain you won't need any of that here."

"Perhaps we should speak with Mr. Hewett," Tanner tried. "There seems to be a misunderstanding as to my role."

The butler affixed him with a steely eye, reminding

him a little of Stephen Roth, the oldest of his friends to remain in England. "Mr. Hewett has already conveyed his wishes to me on the matter. You will find, Mr. Tanner, that he has a particular way of doing things and does not like his routine disturbed. And neither do I."

Tanner thumped his fist against his chest. The butler frowned.

"Sorry," Tanner said. "That is how we recognize our superiors in Batavaria."

He did not so much as smile. "You will be sent for when you are needed."

He glided out of the room so smoothly that Tanner tipped his head to make sure the fellow wasn't on wheels. Then he straightened and dropped his satchel on the bed. It didn't bounce.

"Welcome, indeed," he muttered.

Very likely he was expected to sit on that hard bed as he waited. He had grown used to waiting along the wall as his sovereign attended state functions. But the King of Batavaria had never hidden him away in a cupboard. Neither had Lady Belfort.

So, he used the cold water in the pitcher to rub the travel dirt from his face. No time to shave, though only a little scruff was growing after this morning. Besides, he was a bodyguard, not the lady's suitor.

You could be.

He shook the odd thought away. If he wanted Mr. Hewett to see him as worthy of his trust and recommendation, he would have to be very, very careful not to show how much he already admired his charming daughter. He was a bodyguard. That was all.

But he couldn't do his job with no line of sight, no chance of hearing. Surely Mr. Hewett would understand that.

He thought about using the main stairs but decided not to flaunt the house rules any more than necessary.

Squeezing his way down the servant's stairs, he checked each floor for the layout and security. The floor immediately below his was mostly bedchambers, spaced much farther apart and far better appointed. One room done all in green and overlooking the garden was clearly a withdrawing room. The next floor down held a library, dining room, and withdrawing room. Raised voices echoed out of the last room, urging him forward.

It was a gentleman's study, with a massive desk in the middle surrounded by deep, brown leather chairs and framed maps from around the empire on the paneled walls. The scent of pipe tobacco lingered.

"It's an important decision, marriage," Mr. Hewett was saying from his spot near a window overlooking the front of the house. "Too important to be left to chance."

Julia, standing by the wood-wrapped hearth and now dressed in a pretty green frock, narrowed her eyes at him. "And you think my intelligence and education have in no way equipped me to make a choice that has nothing to do with chance?"

Now her father's eyes narrowed, a far more intimidating look. Her eyes were a warm brown. His were a cool blue. Even his red hair was a lighter shade than hers. And the mustache under his short nose bristled with indignation.

"What do you mean," he said slowly, "education?"

Tanner stiffened at the tone and scolded himself.

Julia snorted. "My tutelage by various governesses, dancing masters, language instructors, musicians, and painters."

Her father relaxed. "Oh, that. Well, they may have taught you all the arts required of a lady, but I doubt they taught you how to find the right lord."

He was determined to thwart her. By the way her head came up, Julia intended to match him.

But another movement caught his eye. The white-haired woman who served as Julia's companion was tiny enough that she nearly disappeared into the armchair in one corner. She had an improbable name of Mrs. Daring, if he recalled. At the moment, she looked as if she wanted nothing more than to escape the escalating conflict.

"I already found the perfect lord," Julia told her father. "Someone dashing and considerate and intelligent, who thinks I walk on water."

Her father chuckled. "Well, that's a start at least. Duke, marquess, earl?"

"An Englishman whose family goes back before the Conquest," she assured him.

He leaned against the windowsill. "The name, my girl."

"Viscount Westerbrook."

Red flamed into her father's cheeks until they clashed with his hair. "No."

She clenched her fists, and Tanner wouldn't have been surprised if she counted to ten before answering him.

"Yes. He is my choice. The sooner you accept that, the better for us both."

"No," her father repeated, crossing his arms over his chest. "He's a weak-willed spendthrift with no ambition."

"He knows his own mind," she insisted, taking a step forward. "If he spends money, it's because he has money and the exquisite taste to use it well. And he doesn't need ambition. He's reached the pinnacle of achievement."

"Ha! That's just a fancy way of saying he's too lazy to move forward."

Now her fists reached her waist. "You didn't complain when he invested in your railroad."

"I don't mind taking money from fools," he said complacently. "I just don't want them marrying my daughter." He pushed off from the sill. "Think, Julia. I've arranged to put the world at your feet. Don't throw it away on a good-for-nothing with a pretty face and a fast horse."

"Very well," she said, and the hair rose on the back

of Tanner's neck. He had heard danger coming many a time. This was it.

"Then I'll marry Mr. Tanner instead," she declared. "After all, he's already compromised me."

CHAPTER TWO

WHAT HAD SHE done! The fire in her father's eyes as he looked toward the doorway told Julia that Tanner had witnessed her dreadful display of temper. And this after making him promise to keep their connection a secret!

But how else was she to respond to her father's highhandedness? He'd refused her any choice in her future! Truly, it was not to be borne.

She squared her shoulders and glanced to Tanner in the doorway. He at least knew how to control his emotions, for his face betrayed nothing of what he might be feeling. He merely stood, watching, waiting. And she wanted to dash to his side and ask him to go along with the statement, only until she knew her next steps.

"Out," her father barked, and her gaze jerked back to him. For a moment, she thought he was giving Tanner the sack, but his gaze was aimed at her. "Mrs. Daring, escort your charge to her room. I'll speak to you both later. Tanner, a word."

"Father," Julia started, not entirely sure what to say to him.

He held up his hand. "Not now."

His lips were a tight line, his color livid. Oh, but she'd done it this time. She picked up her skirts and swept toward the door, Daring hurrying beside her.

Tanner inclined his head as they passed, and all she

could do was beg him with her eyes. Was that a smile? Something like a smile? She wouldn't know until her father came to speak with her.

"Well," she said as her companion shut the door soundly behind them, "I made a mess of that."

"It is never easy attempting to explain your position to someone known for being unreasonable," Daring said. She had a way of talking that was more breath than sound, as if a breeze bore her thoughts. "But perhaps a little more restraint and truthful speaking would have been advised."

Julia paused to glance back. Garrison had wisely taken himself off elsewhere, as had the other servants. What was to stop her from listening at the door?

"It was the truth," she admitted. "Tanner was the one I met in the garden at the Duchess of Wey's ball this summer. While neither of us did anything wrong, some might call a moonlit discussion alone with a gentleman compromising."

"Oh," Daring said, voice even more breath. "I see. Well, then. Come with me."

Julia frowned at her. From the time her mother had grown ill, when Daring had entered her life, she had thought the lady strikingly ill-named. She was tiny, her hair was white and beginning to thin, and her hands constantly fluttered unless they were anchored in some task. Still, she had been a compassionate, caring companion, not at all given to commands.

Now she toddled purposely down the corridor toward the back of the house. With one last glance at the study door, Julia followed.

"It truly isn't so terrible," she tried explaining as Daring paused before the library door and glanced both ways. "You remember that night. Father had been beastly, insisting I could only dance with a duke, as if any would be in attendance besides the duchess's husband."

"A dreadful row," Daring acknowledged, slipping into the library. "The sheer volume left me trembling."

As most things left her trembling, this was not unexpected. Julia was merely surprised she didn't balk entering the shadowed room, where every wall was covered with floor-to-ceiling bookcases or dark-wood paneling.

Daring crossed the thick brown carpet to the wall that backed against the study. "I know you were upset that night. Such a cruel dictate to be unable to dance when you love it so. You are like a butterfly on the meadow on the dancefloor. I'm sure I've said so many a time."

"You have," Julia said with a smile as Daring pulled open one of the glass-fronted bookcases. "And you're right. The injustice of it grew too much. So I ventured out into the garden to try to calm myself, and I was overcome."

Hand on one of the volumes, Daring glanced at her. "And then came Mr. Tanner."

"Yes," Julia admitted. "Just when I thought my heart might break, a cloaked gentleman appeared, as if from the darkness itself. He sat beside me on a stone bench and asked how he might be of assistance. I know I should have sent him away or gone back to the ballroom, but he was so kind."

"And handsome," Daring said, gaze returning to the shelf as she pushed aside this book and that.

Julia's cheeks warmed. "Well, yes, I suppose so. But that wasn't quite so evident in the moonlight. All I knew was that I had been given an ally. It was terribly gratifying."

"Is that why you danced with him at the assembly last month?" Daring asked, handing her a volume.

"To thank him," Julia said, setting the book on the closest side table. "Yes, of course. I didn't think beyond that."

"Words, I fear, that may be inscribed on your gravestone if you don't take greater care," Daring chided.

Julia cocked her head as her companion pulled down two more books, weaved a moment as if the weight was almost too much, then set them carefully aside. The back of the bookshelf was missing, and the remaining paneling was lighter than the rest of the room.

"What have you done?" Julia asked.

Daring stepped out of her way and pointed at the spot. "If I lean in and put my ear just there, I find I can generally hear everything from the study fairly well."

Julia blinked, then smiled as she straightened. "Why, Daring, how very bold of you! I had no idea you listened in on Father's dealings."

"Only when absolutely necessary," Daring assured her. "And when the topic of conversation involves someone dear to me. Now, hurry! I don't know how much we may have missed."

Julia had to bend a little to match her companion's height, but she leaned in and set her ear to the paler paneling. Sure enough, she could hear her father's voice clearly through the wall.

"When the time is right," he said. "Until then, I expect you to treat Julia with all the respect she deserves, and we'll see how things turn out."

He sounded rather chipper for a man who'd just been told the bodyguard he'd hired to keep suitors away from his daughter had already compromised her.

Just what had he and Tanner agreed on?

"I never compromised your daughter," Tanner had said to his employer the moment the lovely Julia had decamped with her companion. He couldn't blame her for throwing down the gauntlet. Her father should have considered her wishes before dismissing the viscount out of hand. Then again, perhaps Hewett knew something more about the fellow than Julia did.

"Do you swear it?" Hewett demanded.

Tanner pressed his fist to his chest. "On my honor and the honor of my country, I so swear."

The man nodded, then motioned him into one of the two chairs closest to the desk. Tanner hesitated.

"Oh, sit," he commanded, doing the same himself. "We might as well be comfortable while we decide whether it's pistols at dawn."

He had no idea what he suggested. He would likely end up dead in any sort of duel with Tanner. Tanner was trained in pistol, rifle, sword, knife, and fisticuffs. Roth insisted they practice daily. Hewett's growing paunch suggested he hadn't practiced anything more than eating, even if he had taken training at some point.

"I prefer the short sword," Tanner said, but he took a seat in the other chair.

Hewett eyed him. "Noted. But I don't think it will come to that. She's lying, isn't she?"

Calling his employer's daughter a liar didn't seem safe either. Best to come clean. If she did not hold herself to their agreement earlier, he had no reason to do so.

"When the Crown Prince of Batavaria and his brother, Count Montalban, visited the Duke of Wey this summer," Tanner began, "my duty was to patrol the area and make sure no mischief was fomenting. I thought it better to stay closer to the house during the duchess's ball because of the number of people in attendance. I came across your daughter in the garden, sobbing."

Hewett stiffened. "Sobbing? Why? Who'd had the temerity to hurt her?"

Again, he had to go carefully. "I offered my help, and she mentioned that she had had an argument with her father before coming and the matter weighed heavily on her."

His face softened. "You might not know it from her bravado, but Julia has always had a gentle heart. I'm sorry I made her cry. That was never my intention. You'll understand when you have children one day, my lad. A father only wants the best for them."

His father had had a very different outlook, but he knew it best not to mention it. He never came off well compared to his illustrious father.

"Of course," he said.

Hewett rubbed his hands together. "So, one moment of kindness in a dark garden. Doesn't sound like such a compromise to me."

Tanner drew a breath. "Only the strictest of hostesses would see it as such."

He nodded. "And the Duchess of Wey isn't nearly so strict. Fine lady. Cavalry officer's widow. Always struck me she knew what's what."

She had struck Tanner the same way.

Hewett leaned forward. "So, here's what we're going to do. I'll go along with this pretense, claim the two of you ought to be engaged."

Tanner kept himself from reacting with the barest of control. "Engaged?"

"That's what happens if a girl is compromised—an engagement or pistols, er, swords, at dawn. Since we've agreed not to go stabbing each other, an engagement should work to my advantage."

He didn't remember coming to that agreement, but the engagement concerned him more. "I do not wish to marry your daughter."

Hewett opened his mouth, then shut it, frown gathering. "Why?" he finally demanded.

This discussion would be the death of him. "Miss Hewett is a lovely lady, and any gentleman would feel fortunate to pay her court. But you hired me to be her bodyguard. I take my oath seriously. Besides, I had hoped this assignment might help advance my career. Marrying any lady would get in the way of that."

Hewett's frown didn't ease. "Career, eh? You see yourself advancing from bodyguard?"

"I see myself acting as bodyguard under more interesting circumstances," Tanner allowed. "Bodyguard to an heiress, particularly outside of the London Season, should not present much of a challenge."

Hewett shook his head. "It's not all ballrooms and visiting, you know. Julia is a bruising rider. You'll be hard-pressed to match her. She's also involved with a number of charities that take her all over the county, and she's organizing a balloon ascension for next week, right here on the estate."

That could be more interesting than he'd expected. "Is she going up in the balloon?"

"I'm not sure on that score," Hewett admitted. "It's more in the way of a scientific experiment. She met Lord and Lady Worthington in London, and they needed a place with water to practice something or some such. Julia will have all the details. There's sure to be a crowd, though, so you'll be needed."

Crowds always added to his work. A bodyguard could never be certain who was among them and what mischief was planned.

"And there's my railway," her father continued, buttons on his waistcoat winking as he puffed out his chest. "First line in Surrey, due to be opened within the fortnight. She'll be by my side as we take the first ride. You'll want to be in on that, I'm sure."

He couldn't argue there. He'd read about the new steam locomotives, but they'd mostly been used in colliers and mines thus far. To ride on one of the first public trains would be something.

"I'll speak to her about her plans for the next fortnight,"

he promised. "But as far as you know, there are no threats to concern us?"

"Not entirely."

Tanner eyed him. Roth had taught him the trick, and though his brown eyes and glower were not nearly as dark as the other guard's, Hewett shifted under them. Then he drew in a breath as if making a decision. Rising, he went to a box on the mantel, returning to offer Tanner a folded piece of parchment.

"I know we spoke a fortnight ago, but I had decided Julia didn't need a bodyguard after all. And then this came the other day."

Tanner opened the note. *You are obstructing my future. Stop now, or you will not like the consequences.*

"Who sent this?" he asked, glancing up.

Hewett shrugged. "I have no idea. The higher you rise, the more enemies you make along the way. I don't fear for myself, mind you. But it's well known that I dote on my daughter. Someone who wants to hurt me could well decide to do it through her."

"Possibly. But the threat isn't specific, either in what you have done to earn the person's wrath or what is to be done about it."

"Doesn't make me any less worried for my girl," Hewett said, resuming his seat. "Julia is everything to me. I just wish I knew who was issuing threats."

"We have some clues." Tanner held the paper up to the light from the window. "Good paper, cut carefully to avoid the watermark that might give away its provenance. Firm handwriting, no spelling or grammatical errors. All that would suggest a gentleman of wealth and education."

Hewett stuck out his lower lip. "Smart lad. But there are still too many fellows in that camp. And I don't think we can rule out the ladies who might be jealous of her good fortune. After all, it wasn't addressed to me."

Tanner brought the paper to his nose. Was that a whiff of sandalwood? It was a common men's cologne. For all he knew, it might have come from the butler or the man standing in front of him.

"How did this arrive?" he asked, lowering the note.

"It was in among the post," Hewett said, "but it carried no postmark, so I doubt it came by mail coach to Weyton."

"Someone slipped it in along the way," Tanner mused.

"Either in the village when my footman went to retrieve it or here while the rest of the mail sat on my desk. You can see why I might be concerned."

He could indeed. Whoever had issued the threat was far too close.

Tanner handed the note back to him. "I'll be doubly on my guard. But I still don't see why I must engage myself to your daughter to protect her."

He leaned forward. "Because, my lad, if you're engaged to her, you can keep any other fellow from getting too close. You can also watch to make sure she doesn't use this so-called engagement to connive her way into a real engagement with that Westerbrook chap."

"Viscount Westerbrook," Tanner said. "She favors him."

His mustache curled on one corner. "And I fail to see why. She can do better. And she will, so long as she doesn't let that temper of hers get in the way of her own good sense. You play along, and you keep her safe. And I'll do what I can to find you a more challenging assignment when this is all over."

What he was asking verged on dishonorable. Honor was the coin of the realm among the Imperial Guards. Tanner's friend, Finn Huber, believed in it above all else, and Roth wasn't far behind. Yet now that Tanner knew Julia might truly be in danger, how could he refuse her father? If he argued, Hewett might well discharge him and hire someone who didn't have his skills. Julia's life was no price to pay for safeguarding his honor. And if he succeeded in protecting her, a more exciting future might be his.

"Very well," he said. "But I will not lie to your daughter any longer than necessary. As soon as possible, I will tell her the truth."

Hewett nodded slowly. "When the time is right. Until then, I expect you to treat Julia with all the respect she deserves, and we'll see how things turn out."

Julia feared she might have to pry information out of her father as to his conversation with Tanner, but he came to her suite a short time after the two of them had finished talking. Indeed, she and Daring had barely replaced the books and scrambled up the stairs before they heard footsteps behind them. They rushed into her lovely blue and white sitting room and dove into the two wingback chairs near the fire.

Daring snatched up the pillowcase she had been embroidering and began plying her needle with far more enthusiasm than the piece usually elicited. Julia grabbed the book she had been reading and held it up as she sank onto the other chair, where she could see the door.

Someone rapped on the panel.

"Come in," Julia called.

She'd prided herself on her calm, cool tone. But Daring dropped the embroidery on her lap and fluttered her hands to wheeze, "Book!"

Oh, my! She quickly turned her book right-side up as her father strolled into the room.

"Just thought you'd want to know that your Mr. Tanner and I came to an understanding," he said, going to take up the poker and nudge the coals in the hearth. "Since he's compromised you, it stands to reason that you should be engaged."

The book slid from her fingers to thud into the Aubusson carpet.

CHAPTER THREE

A S IF HE hadn't heard Julia's gasp, her father turned to offer her a smile. She thought her answering smile was likely rather ghastly. Daring's was positively glued to her face.

"Oh, how lovely," Julia managed. "When are we speaking to the vicar about reading the banns?"

Her father tutted. "Now, then, no girl of mine is going to have her name read out to all and sundry. I'll make sure your fellow gets a special license when we're ready. But with all that's happening with my business and your activities, I'm sure you understand that might be a while yet. Investors grow skittish when they see changes, of any sort."

She wasn't sure why his investors would care when she announced an engagement, though perhaps a few would wonder at her choice when her father had bragged she'd snare no less than a duke.

"Of course, Father," she said dutifully, trying to think of a way out of the predicament. "Though I suppose, with us engaged, it would be prudent for propriety's sake to send Mr. Tanner back to Rose Hill instead of having him stay here."

"Nothing of the sort," her father said, moving closer. "Now he has even more reason to act as your bodyguard. Not that we'll call him that. Might look odd."

The entire thing looked odd as far as she was concerned. "Then what is his role?"

"He'll still escort you out of the house and attend you when anyone calls. If we're invited to dinners or balls, I'll make sure he receives an invitation as well. As far as the world knows, you're a happily engaged couple. You just happen to have a future husband who knows his way around a sword."

"So high on my list of expectations in a groom," Julia drawled.

Her father leveled a finger at her. "Now, none of that, my girl. You're the one who claimed connection with the fellow. I'm just following through in a way that keeps you safe. We'll dine early tonight. Be downstairs by half past five."

He strode out.

Julia sucked in a breath through her nose.

"You did quite well," Daring said, taking up her embroidery once more. "You only baited him once. I do believe you are progressing."

Not if it meant meekly accepting her father's orders. At the moment, however, she needed to know what Tanner thought of all this. Much as she was grateful he apparently hadn't contradicted her story, she had to make sure he knew she didn't intend to marry him. Surely, together, they could find a way to turn this engagement to their advantage.

She came downstairs with Daring at a quarter past, hoping to catch him before her father arrived. Unfortunately, her father was already in residence. They did not stand on ceremony when it was just the three—now four—of them. They did not change for dinner unless they'd been doing something strenuous, and they met in the dining room rather than the more formal withdrawing room next to it. Her father was already seated in his harp-backed chair at the head of the long walnut table, though he rose when she and Daring entered.

She took her usual spot on his right, with Daring across from her, but she couldn't help noticing the place setting beside hers, the delicate white plate and gleaming silverware a contrast to the dark wood.

"Only the best for my future son-in-law," her father joked as if he'd seen her look.

She just had to make sure that statement applied to Lord Westerbrook.

Tanner came in then. He'd changed into a navy coat and buff trousers, with a waistcoat shot with green and gold. He paused inside the doorway as if surveying the scene, then chose a seat next to Daring.

"You're in the wrong chair, my lad," her father informed him. "You should be next to Julia."

"I prefer the view from here," he said, his frank gaze bringing warmth to her cheeks. "I can see both doors as well as all in the room."

Well, and here she'd thought he'd just wanted to watch her!

The footman hurried to rearrange the table.

Her father's presence made it challenging to have any sort of private conversation. He launched into a discussion of his various properties, and Tanner listened intently, as if he thought he might be quizzed on the matter. A lady could only do so much with her eyes before the gentleman must begin wondering about her sanity.

Then, instead of burying himself in his study after dinner as he usually did, her father insisted on everyone adjourning to the upstairs withdrawing room, where he encouraged her to play something on the pianoforte. It was all terribly polite and civilized, and she wanted to scream.

"I asked Mr. Garrison which room he had been given," Daring murmured as the two of them climbed the stairs to bed at a very early hour. "He was lodged in the servants' quarters, but he's been moved to the room next door to your father."

Julia didn't have to ask who she meant, but she didn't see what good the knowledge did her. She certainly wasn't going to call on Tanner in his room. She might actually find herself forced to marry him!

"How nice he's close," she said to Daring before entering her suite, and staying there.

It was the same the next morning. Tanner was already in the breakfast room when she came in, earlier than was her wont. So was her father.

"Lovely day," he caroled. "You'll be attending church this morning, I'm sure."

Julia brightened. "Yes, of course, Father. And before that, perhaps a turn about the rear lawn. Tanner, dear, would you accompany me?"

"Delighted," he said, inclining his head.

"I'll come too," her father declared, tossing down his napkin. "Just the thing to get the blood moving."

That would never do! "But, Father," Julia improvised, "you promised last night to speak to Daring about the troubles she's been having."

Daring coughed and hurriedly raised her napkin to her lips as her face turned as white as her hair.

Her father frowned. "Troubles? I don't recall any troubles."

The napkin fluttered as Daring lowered it. "It's nothing, really, only a little financial difficulty arising from the estate of my dear, late husband. I hadn't intended to impose on you, sir, but your reputation for business acumen is greatly to be admired. Still, I'm sure you have more pressing matters to attend to than the financial wellbeing of a faithful retainer of many years' service." She lowered her gaze and sniffed.

"Oh, very well," her father said. "What's the problem?"

Daring's gaze jerked up. "I could not possibly discuss it publicly!"

He heaved a sigh. "My study. A quarter hour." He pointed a finger at Julia. "You and your betrothed may walk in plain view of the house for no longer than that. Then we're leaving for services."

"Yes, Father," Julia said. She rose, and Tanner followed her out.

She made sure to speak of nothing important until they were safely out of doors, her in her quilted serpentine pelisse and mink muff and him in a heather-colored multi-caped greatcoat. Clouds hung heavy over the estate, the grey mirrored in the waters of the lake. A brisk breeze tugged at her velvet bonnet.

"I have no intention of marrying you," she said, tucking her hands into the silk-lined muff in front of her.

He shrugged, setting his capes to swaying. "I did not think that you did. You were angry with your father. I was merely a means to an end."

Put that way, she sounded entirely devious, perhaps even a little childish.

"I didn't think," she confessed. "And I suppose I expected him to keep arguing. I certainly didn't expect him to betroth us."

The tassels on his boots swung as he moved across the damp grass. "I understand in England it is a lady's choice to call off the engagement. You are free to do so any time."

She hugged the warmth of the muff closer. "Father wouldn't hear of it. If I wasn't engaged to you, he might try to engage me to someone else. So, I suppose there is a benefit to our betrothal."

Another thought struck. "Oh! But if Father thinks we're engaged, he'll stop fretting about Lord Westerbrook. I can contrive to bring the two of them together more often, and Father can see his better qualities. Then, when

I release you from our betrothal, Lord Westerbrook will be the natural choice to take your place."

He said nothing.

"Would it be too much of an inconvenience?" she tried, glancing his way. His gaze was moving from the lawn to the lake to the trees beyond, watching for any trouble. "At least they gave you a better room. I had no idea they were going to put you in the servants' quarters. That hardly seems right for a soldier of your distinction."

"Your father pays me, just as he pays them," he said.

Julia stopped on the lawn. "*Does* he still pay you? I hadn't thought of that either! I certainly wouldn't want to put you in a difficult position."

He stopped to regard her, face once more neutral. "Claiming I compromised you seems to have done that already."

She sighed, shoulders tight. "Oh, Mr. Tanner, I am truly sorry. I'll go to Father right now, tell him it was all a slip of the tongue."

"Too late," he said, returning his gaze to their surroundings. "I confessed to our meeting in the duke's garden. Your father isn't likely to let me off the hook. The best we can do for the moment is continue as he suggested. Sooner or later, he'll grow tired of me. And by then, your viscount might be ready to propose."

The tightness in her shoulders eased. "Thank you. I appreciate this more than you can know. We'll be a happily engaged couple to the world, but I will tell Lord Westerbrook the truth."

And hope he understood.

She looked so relieved he could not tell her the truth, that her father knew all. Color was returning to her cheeks, a rosy red at odds with her hair, which was just visible inside her satin-lined bonnet. He wanted to be glad to have been of service, yet their entire arrangement felt wrong. At times, he had had to keep quiet about a danger to prevent his charge at the moment from panicking. Keeping quiet about this agreement with her father might not be the same thing, but it had the same effect—protecting her. Why did something in him protest?

He forced the matter from his mind as they approached the church that morning. As bodyguard, he rode with the coachman, Mr. Towser, while Mr. Hewett, Julia, and Mrs. Daring sat inside. A wagon followed with the staff. Ahead, the golden stone chapel with its tower at one end looked decidedly sure of itself, as the toll of the bell called the villagers to worship. From what he'd seen, everyone in the area from the Duke of Wey and his family to the least laborer attended. With so many people moving about, it would be easy for danger to creep closer. And Tanner knew from experience how many hiding places the church had.

He had attended with Lady Belfort since she had become his patroness. Two sets of box pews flanked a center aisle leading to a simple cross, but there was a loft on two sides as well as a vestry. Most of the seats were filled, and more than one gaze was trained their way, but nowhere did he spot obvious animosity.

Julia's father led their group to a pew not far behind that of the Duke of Wey, who was attending with his wife, youngest daughter, and her husband. Tanner recognized some of the others in attendance as well, having observed them at the duchess's ball, been introduced to them at the recent assembly, or met them through Lady Belfort, who was visible in all her lavender glory on the other side of the aisle. The dark-haired lady appeared to adore the color, for he had never seen her wear any other.

Beside her, his friend Adrian Keller tipped up his chin,

and Roth nodded a greeting. It was good to know he had reinforcements if needed.

The service was uneventful, the vicar booming out a sermon about what it meant to have charity toward one's neighbor. It was only afterward, as they exited the building, that he had to spring into action.

He saw the danger coming before Julia did. Putting his hand to her elbow where she was walking with Mrs. Daring, he bent to murmur, "Bees heading our direction."

Her eyes widened in alarm.

"Julia, dear," Mrs. Bee called, nearly knocking the minister aside to reach her. "How well you look! We must talk."

Others began beating a strategic retreat. Small wonder. Mrs. Bee was large and bold and ensured every gaze found its way to her. Her husband, whom he had yet to meet, had made his fortune in trade, and she had ensured that their two daughters could profit from their newfound wealth. Today, they all wore fine frilly dresses covered by velvet short jackets, and their hats each had three ostrich plumes curling over the top.

"Your father wishes your company, Miss Hewett," Tanner said with a nod to the lady and her daughters. "Excuse us."

He deftly moved Julia around a headstone, preventing Mrs. Bee from following.

"Oh, that was well done," Julia said with a grin his way. "How did you know?"

"The Bees and I have traded barbs before," he confessed. "Lady Belfort does not enjoy their company."

"Not many enjoy their company," Julia agreed. "Dare I ask who's winning in your contest?"

"My honor prevents a response," he said.

She laughed. Had the sun come out? He could not otherwise explain the warmth that followed.

Mrs. Daring reappeared at her side, and he could only

admire how well she had avoided being ensnared, but then, perhaps Mrs. Bee didn't consider a companion worthy of her attention. With her were Lady Belfort, Keller, and Roth. His colleagues moved with the confident grace expected of the Batavarian Imperial Guard. And why not? Their king had chosen them to be his most trusted agents, protecting him and his two sons until the time when his exile ended and he could go home.

But home had long ago ceased to be Batavaria to Tanner. Now home was where he hung his weapons, ready for the next adventure.

"Julia," Lady Belfort said, taking her hand. "How are you?" She glanced pointedly at Tanner.

"Well," Julia said with a laugh. "As you can see."

"Better than well," her father declared, coming to join them at the edge of the churchyard. "Has she told you the good news yet?"

He hadn't thought the man would be so public about it. His voice was nearly as loud as the vicar's, and several heads were turning their way. Tanner shifted to hide their view of Julia, who had paled.

"Good news?" Lady Belfort asked, glancing between Julia and her father.

"My Julia and your Mr. Tanner have an understanding. We're not announcing it formally as yet, but with you being a good friend of the family…" He winked at her.

Lady Belfort's dark brows rose.

Julia tugged her pelisse closer. "I'll come see you tomorrow and explain everything, Meredith." She brightened. "Any word from Lord Belfort?"

Lady Belfort's face clouded. "Not recently. But we live in hope."

Her husband had devised the peace agreement that was allowing King Frederick to return to Batavaria after years abroad. Lord Belfort was with the delegation going to have the document signed. But even now, some protested change and sought to undo his good work. Everyone would breathe easier when the agreement had been ratified and Lord Belfort was home.

"He's as clever as you are," Julia said. "I'm certain he'll be back as quickly as he can."

Her father asked her ladyship about her plans for the assembly, and Julia and Mrs. Daring chimed in. Tanner allowed the sounds to wash over him as he watched the dispersing crowds. He caught Roth doing the same and smiled. Surveillance was a habit not easily broken.

Keller slipped in beside him. Of the four of them, he was the youngest, and his boyish good looks and wide blue eyes often caused their enemies to underestimate him.

"You are betrothed?" he asked, frown gathering. "So soon?"

"It is not what it seems," Tanner said. He might be forced to lie to Julia, but there was no point in lying to his friend. "But the arrangement allows me to remain close enough to protect Miss Hewett."

"Ah. Is the work so challenging, then?" he asked, joining them in surveying the area. His gaze appeared to light on the Bees and linger. Clever lad. One should always determine the biggest threat.

"Not at the moment," Tanner said. "But Miss Hewett's father has been threatened."

He'd pitched his voice low on purpose, but Roth's listening ears must have caught at least some of the conversation.

"Threatened?" he asked, moving closer. The oldest of the group, he sometimes forgot he was not their superior. And Tanner had to own that his impressive height, raven hair, and incised features were the most likely to intimidate.

"An anonymous note," Tanner explained, drawing

them both a little farther away from Julia and the others. "Nothing tangible."

"Then you must be vigilant," Roth told him.

"Why, I would never have thought of that," Tanner said. Roth glowered.

He should not tease the fellow. Over the years, the three of them and Finn Huber had become close, though he still felt more comfortable on his own. It had been the one complaint his commanding officers had made of his performance in the Batavarian army.

"He'll be the first to distinguish himself," his last colonel had told Count Montalban as Tanner had stood at attention in the palace, waiting to hear whether he'd be promoted into the elite force of the Imperial Guards. "You won't find a man braver. But he doesn't always obey orders. If we had not been at war, I would have discharged him."

Count Montalban had aimed blue eyes as hard as diamonds at him. "What do you say to that, Captain Tanner?"

"I prefer to rely on myself," Tanner had said. "And I obey orders when I respect the one giving them."

His colonel had flamed. Count Montalban had risen from his throne and extended his hand. "Then we will have no trouble. Welcome to the Imperial Guard, Tanner."

He had followed the count, his brother the Crown Prince, and King Frederick from the mountains of Batavaria to the shores of England. But though he respected the count more than any other he had served under, he still did not like obeying orders or relying on others.

But if he needed help, he knew exactly who to ask. He just hoped it wouldn't come to that.

CHAPTER FOUR

TANNER HAD PLANNED to attach himself to Julia's side when they returned to Hewett House until he knew exactly what was on her schedule for the next week. Count Montalban and some of the other dignitaries he had guarded over the years had been prone to dash off with no warning, but he had a feeling Julia would elevate the practice to a fine art. The more he knew, the better he could protect her. He might even find a moment here and there to take his leisure. It wasn't as if the French were storming the gates.

Instead, Mr. Garrison spoke to him after taking Mr. Hewett's coat and watching the fellow stroll to his study. "A word, Mr. Tanner."

Even those four words seemed more than Garrison wanted to give him.

"We'll be in the upstairs withdrawing room," Julia said before starting to climb the stairs. Mrs. Daring glanced at Tanner, then followed.

"How might I be of service, Garrison?" Tanner asked.

"Now that you are being hailed as Miss Hewett's betrothed," the butler said, "there are certain expectations that must be met, in addition to your lodging."

Garrison had been none too happy about having to relocate Tanner to a room next to Mr. Hewett's and just down the corridor from Julia's. Tanner couldn't stop himself from appreciating the irony.

"I'm doing my best not to enjoy the new room," he told the butler now.

Garrison's impassive face twitched. "Nonetheless, I have been informed that you will require the services of a valet."

Had that been Julia's idea or her father's? Tanner waved a hand. "No need. I've seen to my own needs for years."

"Until you became Miss Julia Hewett's betrothed," the butler insisted. "I have assigned Pepin to assist you. He is awaiting your instruction now." That nose was definitely higher than it should be again.

"Then I suppose I should speak to him. Thank you, Garrison."

Too late he realized the comment could be taken as dismissal. Garrison must have thought as much, for his nostrils flared, and he stalked off down the corridor. With a shake of his head, Tanner went to meet his new valet.

He wasn't sure what to expect, but Pepin turned out to be a lad who hadn't quite reached his majority, if his short stature and beardless chin were any indications. He looked vaguely familiar.

"Let me guess," Tanner said as the youth offered an ungainly bow. "Former pot boy."

Pepin's fair skin pinked as he straightened. "No, sir. I swept out the stables and fed the horses. Mr. Garrison said that because I was familiar with animals, I would be a good choice for a military man." He dropped his gaze and shuffled his feet, as if he expected Tanner to argue.

It was an insult, pure and simple. Tanner might never have managed the king's household, but he knew that outdoor staff seldom became indoor staff, particularly those indoor staff closest to their masters. Other houses where he and the guards had been loaned servants, they'd been taken care of by footmen or the butler himself.

But that wasn't this boy's fault.

"I'm sure we'll be perfect for each other," Tanner told

him. "I don't need much help. Just keep the fires lit when it's cold, polish my boots, and fill the washbasin. And don't touch my weapons. I'll see to them."

Pepin glanced up, eyes shining. "Yes, Mr. Tanner, sir. And may I say, it's an honor."

He recognized the look. He'd gazed at his father the same way. Then again, most of Batavaria had gazed at his father that way. When you had a statue of yourself in the square outside your home, it was difficult for people to do anything less. Awarded the Batavarian Cross for bravery during the Battle of Alseres. Credited with the single-handed rescue of the nuns at Mount Saint Alban. Chosen by the king as the head of his guard.

What would his father have thought to find him here, pretending to be engaged to the woman he was guarding?

Julia had expected her father to be less vocal about her engagement to Tanner, but he must have spread the word because at least three more people had approached to congratulate her before she left the churchyard. And every one of them took a moment to ogle Tanner as if he were some new specimen of cabbage miraculously sprung up in their fields.

Worse, her father seemed in far too good cheer, whistling to himself at moments after he had joined them in the upstairs withdrawing room to read a day-old copy of *The Times*, as if he was quite pleased to have a potential son-in-law who was a bodyguard. And this after insisting she marry nothing less than a duke!

"He's up to something," she told Daring after he'd invited Tanner to join him in his study that afternoon. She was highly tempted to put her ear to the paneling again, but they'd had so little warning to set things back and escape last time she didn't want to chance it without a more urgent need.

"Very likely," Daring said complacently, stitching contentedly at her pillowcase. "Though he did give me some excellent advice on where to put my funds on the Exchange."

"At least you've benefited from our charade," Julia said with a smile. "As it is, I will have to call at Rose Hill tomorrow and explain the situation. I do not like Meredith thinking I would jump so quickly into a betrothal."

"You'll have to take your body… betrothed," Daring pointed out.

"I'll speak to him about it, among other things, as soon as he returns from this discussion with Father," Julia promised.

But she hadn't a chance, for the moment he and her father joined them in the withdrawing room again, Tanner approached her.

"Miss Hewett, a bit of exercise would be most welcome. Another turn about the lawn, perhaps?"

Had he read her mind? No, by the scowl on her father's face, her father had read the riot act to him over some supposed infraction, and Tanner felt the need to unburden himself. She could commiserate.

"Delighted," she said, rising. "Daring, would you accompany us?"

Her companion sighed as she set aside her embroidery. "Of course. But you will pardon me if I fail to keep up with two such healthy young people."

What an accommodating lady. Now, if only Julia could convince her father to be so trusting!

The autumn breeze nipped at their cheeks as they set off across the rear lawn a short while later. A pair of swans honked their way across the sky, aiming for the lake. The trees were nearly bare now, reaching skeleton fingers toward each other as if lonely.

"What did you and my father find to talk about?" Julia asked as she strolled along beside Tanner.

He grimaced, pausing to kick a pebble out of the way of his black, tasseled boots. "He wanted a report on who had approached you at church before he joined you."

Julia pulled up short. "He wanted you to spy on me!"

Daring, who had been walking a few steps behind, tsked as she too was forced to stop or run into them. "And I had thought that my role."

Julia shook her head. "That's no one's role. If he has a concern over my acquaintances, he can discuss the matter with me directly."

"Which is what I suggested," Tanner said.

Julia reined in her temper. "Good," she said, setting off once more. "And I will not ask you to relay a message to him. I will talk to him at first opportunity."

Tanner inclined his head. "In the meantime, I had hoped to speak with you in any regard. If I am to protect you, I must know your plans."

Daring laughed, then turned the sound into a cough.

Julia cast her a look. "What? I plan."

"You do," Daring allowed. "On occasion. When necessity compels."

"I plan," Julia told Tanner emphatically, facing forward again. "In fact, I am planning to visit Rose Hill tomorrow. We can return Lady Belfort's horse. And Tuesday is my at-home day, so callers are sure to come to the house."

"Or at least such callers as may be had here in Surrey," Daring put in with a sigh.

"And what about this balloon ascension?" Tanner asked.

Excitement bubbled up inside her, and she clasped her hands in front of her pelisse. "Oh, yes! We have much to do before Friday. Lord and Lady Worthington will be visiting us with their latest experiment. I can hardly wait!"

He cocked his head. "These Worthingtons, are they related to Petunia, Lady Ashforde?"

"In a way," she said, lowering her hands. "Her sister-in-law, Charlotte, Lady Bateman, is the sister of the current Lord Worthington. Have you met?"

"Lady Bateman, yes, when I assisted in guarding Lady Ashforde before her marriage."

"Oh, of course! So you have experience playing bodyguard to ladies." Julia grinned at him. "How fortunate I am."

He chuckled as they approached the stables. "I have protected several ladies over the years. Lady Giselle, the daughter of one of King Frederick's courtiers. Lady Francesca, wife of the count who offered us shelter in Italy."

Now, why did she have a desire to nudge both ladies into the lake? "How interesting! Until now, Daring has been my protection."

"And it has been a long, thankless role," Daring said with another sigh.

"Now, I'm certain I thank you," Julia protested. "And I will thank you too, Tanner, for your attentions."

Oh, but that made it sound as if he were paying her court. Warmth rushed to her cheeks. She was only glad he did not pursue that line of conversation.

"This Lord Worthington," he mused as they passed the stables and turned toward the front of the house. "Is he an adventurer?"

Julia laughed. "No indeed! He is a natural philosopher. So is his wife. They specialize in investigating all aspects of ballooning, and they travel to test their theories. I imagine it's quite the life."

His smile was not so much the lift of his mouth but the light in his eyes. Yet his question proved he was focused on his work. "How many others will attend this ascension?"

"We planned to invite friends from around the area and a few from London," she allowed. "None will be staying with us besides Lord and Lady Worthington. So, if you're concerned about strangers, I can certainly vouch for everyone who will be in attendance."

"Good to know," he said. "You've given me an easy assignment."

She wasn't sure why he didn't sound more pleased about that.

The next morning, after a late breakfast, they met at the front of the house for the drive to Rose Hill. Her father had taken one of the carriages to visit an investor in the area. Garrison had called for the other larger coach, so there would be plenty of room for the three of them. A groom was already leading Meredith's gelding to tie it at the back. Julia simply wasn't sure why Tanner had come armed. He had a short sword in a scabbard strapped to his hip, and she wouldn't have been surprised if the bulge in his jacket was a pistol.

"Do you expect us to be attacked?" she asked as he assisted her into the coach behind Daring.

"It never hurts to be prepared," he said. "I'll ride."

"But you're my betrothed!" Julia protested.

"And therefore all the more determined to protect you," he assured her before shutting the door.

"Well!" Julia huffed, settling into her seat as the carriage set off.

"A gentleman who takes his duty seriously is not to be despised," Daring told her.

Julia turned her gaze out the window.

The road from Weybridge speared down into Weyton until it intersected the river road. Her coachman turned the carriage to run along the Thames, glistening grey to her right through the trees. The sky was just as grey, though here, at least, some of the trees had kept their leaves. The spots of gold and russet stood out in bright patches as they turned onto the long, tree-lined drive to Rose Hill.

The small, stately house with its ornamental pond at the front sat on a slight rise. The estate had been in Lady Belfort's family for generations. Her butler, Mr. Cowls, had the door open for them as she and Daring climbed down from the carriage. With his balding pate and rheumy eyes, he seemed as old as the house itself.

"Miss Hewett, Mrs. Daring," he greeted them. "Always a pleasure to have you with us."

"I believe you have been introduced to my betrothed, Kristof Tanner," Julia said as Tanner brought the gelding next to the house. She had vowed to tell Meredith all, but she couldn't help her little tease. Mr. Cowls was noted for being as unflappable as Fortune, Meredith's cat, was wise. Julia thought she might finally see him discomposed, but he did not so much as blink at her announcement.

"Mr. Tanner," he said with a nod. "Welcome back, and congratulations."

"Ah, but congratulations may be premature, Cowls," Tanner said. "We'll see how long she tolerates me. Are Keller and Roth about?"

"At the cottage," Mr. Cowls replied.

Tanner looked to Julia. "You should be safe here. I'll take this fine mount to the stables and have a word with the other guards."

Julia nodded, and he rode off past the house. Feeling a bit as if he'd taken some of the light with him, she lifted her skirts to step into the entry hall. Like much of Rose Hill, it was paneled in squares of dark wood. Mr. Cowls nodded to a footman, who quickly took her and Daring's coats and bonnets.

"Her ladyship is receiving," Mr. Cowls told them. "Allow me to show you up."

"No need, Mr. Cowls," Julia said, fluffing at her sleeves. "We know the way."

"But I believe your escort is here," he said, training his gaze down the corridor behind them.

Julia turned. From the darkness trotted a grey-coated cat with white around her throat like a cravat. Julia crouched and held out a hand to greet the sweet feline.

Fortune stalked past her and scaled the stairs as if Julia and Daring did not exist.

Mr. Cowls frowned.

So did Julia as she rose. Fortune's attentions were prophetic. It was said if she approved of you, your character was very fine indeed. She and Julia had known each other for years and always gotten along famously. Why give her the cut direct now?

They found Fortune with her mistress, cuddled on the sofa as if claiming pride of place. The Rose Hill withdrawing room was far cozier than either withdrawing room at Hewett House, the furnishings done in rose and grey, and the sofa and chairs comfortable enough to dispose one to stay and chat. She had heard that Meredith had redecorated when she and her husband had purchased her childhood home from the cousin who had inherited.

"Good morning, Julia," her friend said now with a smile, one hand on her fashionable lavender skirts. "And Mrs. Daring."

Daring dropped a curtsey. "Your ladyship." She scurried to a chair at the edge of the grouping and settled her grey skirts.

"Good morning to you too," Julia said, going to take the chair closer to the sofa. "Forgive the early hour. Father's announcement at church yesterday has been weighing on me, and I wanted to explain, at least to you. Tanner and I are not engaged."

To her surprise, Fortune hissed, dropped down from the sofa, and disappeared behind it.

"She is in the oddest mood," Julia said, frown returning. "Have I done something to offend her?"

"I fear only you can answer that question," Meredith said. "But you were saying that you and Tanner are not engaged. Why is your father claiming otherwise?"

Julia made a face. "He was absolutely unreasonable the other afternoon, going so far as to tell me who I was allowed to wed. To spite him, I claimed that Tanner had compromised me."

Meredith raised her dark brows. "Indeed."

Her tone seemed to have cooled a few degrees, and the chair felt unaccountably hard all of a sudden. "I shouldn't have. Tanner came to my aid in the garden at the duchess's ball this summer. We only spoke for a few moments. Truly, no one would consider that a compromise."

"Oh," Meredith said, leaning back, "I think you will find that some would be only too happy."

She felt as if a cold wind had blown through the house. "Regardless, I had no business bringing Tanner into the disagreement with my father, who promptly took it upon himself to see us engaged. And the oddest thing is that, after getting over his anger, Father seems pleased as Punch."

"I see," Meredith said, lavender gaze unreadable. "And Tanner agreed to this engagement?"

Julia shifted on the chair. "He agreed to go along with the ruse for now. It should keep Father from foisting another groom on me, at the least."

"So long as you and Tanner are of one mind in this," she replied. "But you must be very careful, Julia, or you could find yourself required to marry your bodyguard."

CHAPTER FIVE

AS COWLS HAD suggested, Tanner found his friends in the cottage down the drive. A miniature version of the bigger house, it was made of the same creamy stone and nestled among a copse of trees. The four guards had been given the use of it, along with a small staff to see to their needs, while Lady Belfort used her considerable influence to find positions for them in England.

Finn Huber had been hired as a bailiff by the Marquess of Kendall to the south and had recently left with his bride to take up their duties. Abigail, Lady Belfort's former companion, would be teaching school. Roth was working as a night guard for a fancy steam manufactory in the area, though he was up and practicing in the yard when Tanner arrived. He lowered his sword and followed Tanner into the house.

Keller joined them in the sitting room off the entry hall. "How goes the engagement?" he asked, dropping onto one of the sofas that flanked the hearth.

Tanner sat on the other. He was tempted to stretch out, but Roth generally took a dim view of relaxing. At any time. Even now, he frowned as Tanner set his sword aside.

"I see little need for it, truth be told," Tanner answered his friend. "If someone is out to hurt Hewett or his daughter, they move very slowly."

"That doesn't mean they aren't moving at all," Roth insisted, grabbing a hard-backed chair and straddling it.

"But I do not understand. Either you are engaged, or you are not."

"Miss Hewett and I met each other at the Duchess of Wey's ball last summer."

"How?" he demanded, sharp grey eyes alert. "You were patrolling."

Keller, who knew the story, merely smiled.

Tanner went on to explain his meeting with Julia in the garden, the way she had goaded her father, and his agreement with Hewett to play the devoted fiancé.

When he finished, Roth leaned back in the chair. "Where is the honor?"

"The honor is in protecting Mr. Hewett and his daughter," Tanner assured them both. "I will do what I must."

Roth frowned at him. As if he sensed trouble brewing, Keller intervened, turning to Tanner even as he turned the conversation. "What more do you know about Miss Hewett's plans?"

"There will be a balloon ascension this Friday," he explained. "The crowd could be large, but Miss Hewett says she can vouch for everyone who will attend."

"Insufficient," Roth said. "Keller and I will join you, so long as I can be free before dark."

He had to clamp his jaws together a moment to prevent a harsh retort. It wasn't a bad idea to have extra eyes at the ascension.

"I cannot be sure when the event will end," Tanner told him, "but leave when you must."

Keller was studying a button on his paisley waistcoat. "And will the Bees attend?"

Tanner chuckled. "Miss Hewett holds them in as low esteem as Lady Belfort does, so I doubt it. But they may be at the railway opening planned for the next fortnight. It sounds like that will be attended by far more people."

"Then we will help there as well," Roth promised.

Keller nodded.

Tanner rose and buckled on his sword belt. "I should return to the house. You may want to join me. There will likely be cakes."

They perked up at that, and the three of them walked back to the house in charity with each other.

Fortune met them on the stairs and escorted them into the withdrawing room, where the ladies greeted them warmly. The cat followed Tanner to a chair and rubbed against his boots.

"She still favors you, I see," Lady Belfort said with a smile.

Tanner smiled too. "You always said she was clever." He bent to run his hand down the soft, grey coat. Fortune slipped away from his fingers and crossed to Julia's side. Then she sat, head high, and copper-colored eyes drilling into Tanner as if daring him to come closer.

But was it Fortune herself or Julia she wanted him to come fetch?

Meredith smiled as her guests and the Imperial Guards chatted. Two of her four fellows were settled, at least for now in Tanner's case. It had certainly taken longer than she'd expected. Generally, she had ideas immediately on where to place one of her clients, and she merely had to wait to see if Fortune approved. She had learned long ago that, though her own impressions of people might be mistaken, Fortune was unerringly correct in her assessment.

Which was why her antipathy toward Julia was such a mystery. Her pet had taken to her fiery young neighbor from the day they'd met. Meredith had been certain that Fortune meant to match Julia with Tanner. Surely this pretend engagement was just the thing to bring them closer together. So why was Fortune suddenly unimpressed with Julia?

Perhaps Meredith had been mistaken in placing Roth at the manufactory without involving her pet, but she hadn't felt comfortable bringing Fortune to such a dangerous place and the owner would not have felt comfortable calling at Rose Hill. Besides, it wasn't as if hearts were involved. Still, Roth did not seem happy in his position. He had ever kept things close, and his firm-jawed face held a tension at the best of times. But now it was as if a burden was weighing on those strong shoulders. She would have to look elsewhere.

And then there was Keller. She watched him now as Tanner teased him about his last disastrous showing at cards. His cheeks were reddening, and he ducked his head. He might not be the best at whist, but he was kind, considerate, and as loyal as they came. By all accounts, he was a fiend in battle. She had thought to have him teach swordplay and fisticuffs at the local boys' school, but the headmaster had deemed him too young. And the employer at every guard position that had arisen so far could not seem to appreciate his skills.

"I can't have him near my weaving girls," the millowner in the next county had written her after she'd sent Keller to see him. "Half of them couldn't keep their eyes off him when he came for the interview. I'd never get a lick of work done if he was here all the time."

Tanner had jokingly offered to break a few bones in Keller's pretty face to solve the problem, and the two of them had tussled good-naturedly. But the issue remained.

She and Fortune would simply have to keep working until all her gentlemen were living happily ever after.

Having assured her friend of the true state of her feelings, Julia departed Rose Hill much relieved, even if

Tanner had insisted on riding on the bench with Mr. Towser, their coachman.

"We should shop," she told Daring as they rode in the carriage back toward Hewett House.

"Do you require a new barrel?" her companion asked. "Or perhaps a different pair of shoes for the horses? I don't recall there being much more in Weyton than a cooper and a blacksmith."

"I have it on good authority there's a new linendraper," Julia told her. She reached up and rapped on the panel. "Towser, we will stop in Weyton."

"Very good, miss," her coachman called down.

Tanner didn't offer a word until she had alighted on his arm.

"Where do you intend to go?" he asked, gaze raking the area as if he expected a brigand behind every window box on the neat, white-washed cottages down the lane.

"There," Julia said with a nod across the street to the new shop. "I understand our linendraper has absolutely lovely ribbons and trimmings."

He regarded her bonnet, which was one of her favorites, a deep blue velvet surmounted with peacock feathers and jet beading. "And you require more?"

Julia laughed at his quizzical tone. "I require different, sir. It would not do to be seen wearing the same old thing."

He chuckled. "While I occasionally indulge in a new waistcoat, my three coats and a dress uniform seem to suffice."

"You are not an heiress whose father must appear as wealthy as Midas," Julia told him. "If I didn't dress well, some might think my father's ventures were lacking."

"So we tell ourselves," Daring muttered.

Julia ignored her.

Tanner glanced up and down the lane, then stepped

away from her. "Wait here." He crossed to the shop and shut the door behind him.

"What is he doing?" Julia asked, trying to see past the bolts of cotton in the front window.

"Securing the perimeter, I should think," Daring said.

She frowned. "Securing the what?"

The door opened, and the vicar's wife hurried out, followed by the blacksmith's oldest daughter. They were so flustered they didn't appear to even notice her or Daring across the street.

"Have a good day, ladies," Tanner said behind them. He held the door open and motioned for her to join him.

"Did you just throw them out?" Julia asked as she and Daring complied.

"I suggested it might be safer for them elsewhere," he said as they entered around him.

"Oh, ladies, thank goodness!" The linendraper, a small, balding fellow neatly decked out in navy and cream, had a hand on the chest of his apron. "For a moment, I thought I was being robbed!"

So, of course she had to buy more than she had intended, just to assure the poor man that all was well.

"You, Mr. Tanner," she said as they left a once-more smiling proprietor, "are an expensive habit."

"I don't know," Daring said, crossing the street at her side. "I am rather pleased with the length of grosgrain I purchased."

"Always happy to help," Tanner said with a smile in her companion's direction.

"And will you evict everyone in any shop we approach?" Julia asked as they reached the coach. "What if I wish to visit with friends in the village? Mrs. Godwin, perhaps, or the Duchess of Wey. Will you throw out their staffs?"

"We can meet the duchess at the castle," Tanner said. "It is always secure. I'm sure we could determine whether this Mrs. Godwin protects her home sufficiently."

Julia snorted. "Why would she? I very much doubt there's a great deal of danger to be had anywhere in Weyton."

"You might be surprised," he said, and she could not get him to elaborate.

He was equally adamant about her safety on Tuesday. Her friends knew it was her at-home day, when she entertained callers. Tanner stationed himself in the entry hall and greeted everyone before allowing Garrison to lead them to the formal withdrawing room, where she and Daring held court. The tight lines of her butler's face told her what he thought of the strategy.

It was also clear that many in the area had heard of her engagement. They were just as keen to get a better look at Tanner.

"But who is his family?" asked Mrs. Godwin, who was one of her first callers that day. "I'm sure I've met him somewhere, but I seldom go up to London." An Amazon of a lady, she was of a different generation from Julia and had lived in the area as long as Meredith, having married one of the wealthiest landowners.

"Mr. Tanner was a member of the Batavarian Imperial Guard," Daring supplied. "Lady Belfort is his patroness."

"Ah, of course." She glanced toward the door. "Does he perhaps have a brother? My Lucy's looking."

Callers came and went much of the afternoon, so she was not surprised to hear the knocker sound again at half past three. The prideful voice that rang from the entry hall was more of a shock.

"Why, Mr. Tanner. How very delightful to find you here. You remember Mr. Tanner, girls? One of Lady Belfort's strapping guards. If you wished to call on neighbors, I do think you might have started with us."

Daring surged to her feet. "I'm certain I left my embroidery upstairs. Excuse me."

"I will not," Julia said, following her. "For I'm leaving too."

"The servant's stair," Daring hissed, and they both darted through the dining room next door and into the serving area and stairs beyond.

Daring shut the door and heaved a sigh. "It must be terribly trying for Mrs. Bee, the way everyone attempts to avoid her."

"I think it more trying for those who cannot escape," Julia said. "How long will we have to wait until she gives up, do you think?"

"Possibly hours," Daring said, voice echoing in the stair. "I'm for a nap."

"Perhaps I'll see what Father is up to." Julia winked at her. "She won't dare approach me in his study."

Daring patted her hand. "Come fetch me when it's safe again."

Her companion headed upstairs, and Julia crossed the landing. She cracked open the door that led onto the main corridor and peered out, but the entry hall was empty of any save Garrison, who was shutting the double doors on the formal withdrawing room as if hoping never to open them again. He must have shut Tanner in as well.

She slipped out and down the corridor for the closed door to her father's study.

But even there, voices stopped her from entering.

"You cannot do this to me." It was a man's voice, a bit high but perhaps it was because of the strain in it. "You'll ruin me."

"You should have thought of that before you invested in canals, my lad. Railways are the future of the Empire. I won't let the opportunity pass just to keep your boats afloat."

"And I'll not let the opportunity pass to pay you back for what you've done."

Angry footsteps sounded, heading in her direction. Julia ducked back into the servant's stair. She slowly counted to five, then peered out again, in time to see a thin-haired fellow accept his hat from Garrison, clap it on his head, and barge out the front door.

Who was he? Was her father actually in danger? Perhaps he should be the one with a bodyguard! And perhaps someone should follow this miscreant and stop him from whatever dastardly plan he hoped to enact.

Tanner would know what to do. But Tanner was in the formal withdrawing room with the dreaded Mrs. Bee and her daughters. She was wracking her brain for a way to separate them when the knocker sounded again.

"Good afternoon, Garrison. Is Miss Hewett at home?"

That voice—so warm and friendly it sent little shivers along her skin. Why should she settle for Tanner when she had Lord Westerbrook?

She took a minute to sleek back her hair and brush off her sleeves before popping out of the stair and sashaying down the corridor.

"Lord Westerbrook, what a pleasant surprise," she said, taking a moment to appreciate the spun gold of his hair, the perfect cut of his bottle-green coat. "Won't you come with me to the library? Garrison, please ask Daring to join us. I believe she's in her room."

Her butler's thin lips twitched as if he were trying not to smile. Why did he find this amusing? "Of course, Miss Hewett. Shall I ask your father to join you as well?"

"No," Julia chorused with her viscount. They both grinned at each other conspiratorially.

"No, thank you, Garrison," Julia amended, forcing her gaze away from his lordship's brilliant blue eyes. "I'll let Father know myself at the appropriate time." She took Lord Westerbrook's arm and drew him down the corridor and into the library, leaving the door open as propriety demanded.

"I didn't think you were coming out until the railway opening," she told him as they ventured to the chairs near the hearth. "What brought you into the wilds of Surrey?"

Before she could sit, he took both her hands in his, lips and eyes turning down. "I was meeting on an investment, but I had to see you. I received the most distressing letter from your father. He claims you are engaged. Please say it isn't so."

How had he allowed himself to be trapped? Tanner tried edging toward the door of the withdrawing room again, only to find Miss Bee the younger there before him, simpering up at him. Her pale blue eyes had a glint in them, not unlike Mrs. Daring's look when acquiring her ribbon.

"I have never known Miss Hewett to keep us waiting," her mother said from the sofa, mulberry-colored skirts swaying as her foot tapped. "If I were her, I would be speaking with my staff."

"That butler always looks as if he thinks he's better than us, Mama," her younger whined before flouncing over to sit beside her.

The elder offered Tanner a more demur smile, hands in the lap of her muslin gown. Of the three, Tanner had found her the least onerous.

"Perhaps we came at a bad time, Mama," she said. "We can call another day."

"Nonsense," her mother said. "We're here now. We merely need Miss Hewett to make an appearance. Although…" she trailed off and looked Tanner up and down for the third time, "I'm sure you can be entertaining when you put your mind to it, Mr. Tanner."

"You honor me, madam," Tanner said, inclining his head. "But I know Miss Hewett will be devastated if she misses the opportunity to chat with you. I'll see what's keeping her."

This time he made it out the doors before one of the Bees could stop him.

He shut them in and turned to eye Garrison, who was waiting by the wall, gaze trained down the corridor toward the library door. "Have you located Miss Hewett?"

He gave Tanner the briefest of glances. "I had no need to locate Miss Hewett. She is entertaining a caller."

Tanner stiffened. "A caller? What caller?"

From the library, a laugh trilled. He stalked in that direction.

CHAPTER SIX

JULIA'S CALLER WAS a gentleman. Was this what the English called a Corinthian? He looked the part of a sporting mad fellow with his tailored coat and gleaming boots. Certainly he had the air of confidence, leaning back in his chair, arms draped along the brown leather and smile amused. In fact, he acted entirely too much at home in Julia's company, even with Mrs. Daring seated a short distance away.

Tanner strode to meet him. "State your name and your business here."

The fellow frowned as if no one had ever spoken to him that way before.

Julia stared at Tanner. "Tanner! That's no way to address a guest in my home."

"Ah, the valiant Tanner." The upstart rose and bowed. "Delighted to meet you, sir, and I must thank you for championing our cause. Julia told me all about your little ruse. I'll make sure you're not overly inconvenienced."

"Father wrote Lord Westerbrook about our engagement," Julia explained. "His lordship had a good laugh when I explained the situation."

His lordship had had a good smirk, and Tanner felt the urge to knock the smile from his handsome face.

"Regardless," he said to Julia, "as your bodyguard, I must be informed about visitors to the house."

"Standard practice," Mrs. Daring muttered before taking another stitch of her ever-present embroidery.

"Bodyguard?" Westerbrook laughed. "Julia needs no bodyguard. I daresay she charms anyone she meets."

Julia beamed at him. "That is so sweet of you to say. Now, I shouldn't keep you, though I so enjoy your company. We cannot upset Father. And I will see you at the railway opening."

"Of course." He took her hand and bowed over it, lips closing in. Mrs. Daring frowned.

Tanner grabbed him by the back of his coat and hauled him upright.

"Oh, I say," he protested, but Tanner marched him toward the door.

"Tanner!" Julia cried, hopping to her feet and following. "Remember your duty!"

"I am," he assured her as Mrs. Daring rose with a martyred sigh. "It is my duty to see this blackguard thrown out of the house." He made a show of winking at the viscount before releasing him.

"Oh, very good," he murmured. He raised his clean-shaven chin and straightened his lapels. "Now, see here, my good man."

"No, you see here," Tanner said, taking his arm and dragging him toward the door. "Julia is my intended, and I'll thank you to save your attentions for a lady who might appreciate them."

"What's all this then?" Mr. Hewett strode out of his study as Garrison handed the viscount his hat and glared at Tanner.

"Just putting out the trash, sir," Tanner said, and he yanked open the door with his free hand, pushed Westerbrook through it, and followed him out.

"Yes, well, that should do it," the viscount said, shaking Tanner off. "Nicely played. He didn't suspect a thing."

"He might be watching from the window," Tanner cautioned. "Best we stay in character."

His lordship's coachman had been walking the horses. Tanner motioned him over, then all but shoved his lordship into the vehicle.

"You're good," Lord Westerbrook said, surreptitiously rubbing at his arm. "But I meant what I said. I'll make sure you are not inconvenienced by all of this. In fact, I'd be delighted to recompense you for any time lost while you deflect suspicion from Julia and me."

"I'm already well recompensed," Tanner told him. "Safe travels back to London." He slammed the door and motioned to the driver to go. The coach trundled down the drive, picking up speed as it went. Tanner stayed on the gravel until the vehicle had turned onto the Weybridge Road.

His fingers seemed to want to stay fisted. He shook them out as he turned for the house.

Mr. Hewett was waiting when Tanner came back in, grin so large it widened his mustache. "Well done, my lad. That's giving him what for."

"Exactly what I would have done," Mrs. Daring agreed.

Julia's smile looked far from pleased.

The doors to the formal withdrawing room were thrown open from within.

"Miss Hewett!" Mrs. Bee caroled, eyes lighting like a cat who had spotted a plump mouse. "*There* you are! You must come and join us. We have so much to discuss."

"So do we," Julia murmured to Tanner before broadening her smile and going to do her duty.

Julia was in no mood to survive a visit with the Bees, but she managed to sit on a chair in the formal withdrawing room and smile at appropriate times. Her father had designed the room to impress, with crimson draperies trimmed in gold fringe on the windows overlooking the drive, silk paper patterned in golden swirls on the walls, and a black marble fireplace surmounted with a massive gilt-framed mirror that reflected back the salon's glory. But the firm horsehair furnishings, for all their velvet coverings, required one to sit up straight and discouraged one from lingering.

Except when that one was Mrs. Bee.

She fluffed at the flaxen curls beside her round face. "This weather! I cannot stomach Surrey in autumn. Drip, drip, drip. I swear it is all I hear some days. However do you survive, Miss Hewett?"

"I find the cool air bracing," Julia said.

"It is more difficult for those of us of a certain age," Daring wheezed.

Mrs. Bee had a tendency to ignore anyone she felt beneath her. "Yes, you and my girls certainly enjoy a romp across the fields," she said to Julia before turning to her oldest. "Elspeth, tell Miss Hewett about your new horse."

The daughter's pale eyes lit. "Oh, she is such a darling, Miss Hewett! Father bought her for me."

"From Tattersalls," her mother put in as if it were important everyone knew he had been to the most famous source of horseflesh in London.

Julia had pity on the girl, who was only a few years her junior. "Is she a goer?"

"She flies!" she enthused. "If Father would allow it, she could even join the hunt."

"Now, then, there will be no talk of that," her mother said with a frown in her direction that sent her closing in on herself again. "A lady riding to the hunt. What rubbish."

Julia knew a number of ladies, of much higher rank, who rode to the hunt, but she decided not to mention the fact. She always felt more in charity with the fox.

"And what will you be wearing at the next assembly?" Daring put in.

Mrs. Bee could not resist answering that question, even if it had come from a woman she considered no better than a servant, and the next little while was passed without anyone coming to fisticuffs or being forced to flee.

Finally, Mrs. Bee stood, and her daughters climbed to their feet as well. "We should be going. We will see you on Friday for the balloon ascension."

Despite Julia's best efforts, her smile slipped. "The balloon ascension?"

"Yes, with Lord and Lady Worthington," Mrs. Bee said as if Julia might have forgotten. "It is only to be expected they'd want to come to Surrey for their attempt. We are the very best of places."

Her daughters nodded agreement.

Three more women at an out-of-doors event were not such an inconvenience, but this was the Bees! So much for Julia's select group!

"Well, we were only planning on a few people attending," she tried. "It is an experiment, so it might not be as exciting as you would expect."

Mrs. Bee waved a hand. "You can find a way to make it exciting for all."

"Mother was certain our invitations had merely been lost in the post," her oldest daughter put in. "That seems to happen a great deal, invitations being lost. I can't count the number of times a hostess has told me of it happening to ours. It must be terribly difficult on arrangements."

"The postal system is notoriously unreliable," her mother lamented.

Daring made an attempt to hold them off as well. "I understand it will rain. And the wind is sure to come up. It is Surrey in autumn, after all, as you so eloquently noted. I only hope I have sufficient fortitude to brave the elements." She shivered.

"I have a fur tippet I'd be happy to loan you," Miss Bee the elder said kindly, "and a muff to match. I find they keep me quite warm indeed. I wouldn't want you to miss something so momentous."

"Indeed," Julia said. She managed to chivvy them toward the entry hall at last.

"Perhaps my nerves will be overcome on Friday," Daring mused after Garrison had seen them out the door.

"Don't you dare leave me alone with them," Julia threatened. She turned to her butler. "Have you seen Mr. Tanner, Garrison?"

"No, Miss Hewett," he said, and he did not seem disposed to go in search. Julia left Daring in the upstairs withdrawing room and went looking herself.

She located her perfidious false fiancé in the kitchen, sitting at the worktable while their cook and her female assistants found ways to work right next to him, their blond heads bobbing in interest to his conversation.

"And then you gave him what for, I'll wager," Mrs. Cheevers said, smacking her cleaver down on a choice bit of beef.

"Between Mr. Huber and me, we managed to send him packing," Tanner allowed. "And he never tried to accost the prince again."

The assistant cook and pot girl stopped their work to applaud.

"What an interesting life you lead, Mr. Tanner," Julia said from the doorway, and the women all quickly dropped their heads and busied their hands. "A word, if it wouldn't inconvenience you."

"You are never an inconvenience," he assured her, rising. He popped the last bit of scone he had been eating into his mouth and followed her out.

On the first floor, she checked to make sure her father

was busy in his study before leading Tanner up to the family withdrawing room. Her waiting companion sank deeper into the sofa as if hoping to be ignored here as well.

"We must speak of your behavior this afternoon," Julia informed him, pacing before the hearth. "What were you thinking? You dragged poor Westie out of the house as if he had been caught stealing the silver!"

His smile was more satisfied than sorry as he went to lean against the hearth. "Westie?"

She raised her chin. "Lord Westerbrook gave me leave to use the nickname he reserves for family and friends."

"How thoughtful."

She wanted to shake the amusement from his voice. "It was. Everything was going well until you barged in."

"I'm supposed to be your betrothed," he pointed out. "You don't think I'd mind coming in to find another fellow kissing your hand?"

The memory brought heat to her cheeks. "I think you entirely overreacted, sir." She stalked to the chair closest to Daring and dropped into it.

"Perhaps," he allowed, taking another chair. "But I have to own it was fun."

That jerked her upright. "Fun!" she sputtered. "Well, I never!"

The twinkle in his eyes was impossible to miss. "I fear you will, frequently, if that's how your viscount is prone to behave. I am your bodyguard."

She opened her mouth to give him what for, when she remembered what had happened in her father's study. "We both know I don't require a bodyguard, but my father may. When I was trying to avoid the Bees, I overheard Father and another man talking. His visitor threatened him!"

"Such poor manners," Daring said, hands fluttering.

Tanner had stiffened. "Who was it?"

"I don't know," Julia admitted. "I only saw the back of him, and I didn't recognize his voice. But he claimed whatever Father was doing would ruin him and vowed to pay him back in kind."

"A gentleman of Mr. Hewett's success is bound to make enemies," Daring lamented.

Tanner nodded. "I'll speak to your father. Do you have need of me at the moment?"

"I'm not certain I have need of you at all," Julia said. "Westie might even have proposed today, if you hadn't interfered."

"In which case, he would be the one speaking to your father. Since he did not, it is left to me." He rose, bowed, and saw himself out.

"Impossible man," Julia muttered, going to sit beside her companion on the sofa.

"But useful," Daring suggested.

Guilt nipped. "Yes, I suppose he is. I hope he can convince Father to take care. And I hope I can convince Father that Westie is a better choice."

"Stand your ground," Daring said, taking up her embroidery. "I wish I'd had your fortitude when I was younger. Things might have turned out differently."

Julia gazed at her. Her white head was bent over her work, her fingers moving slowly. "Why, Daring, did you have to fight off suitors?"

She heaved one of her martyred sighs. "Entirely too many and, I'm ashamed to say, none I took seriously until I met my dear husband. Though there was one fellow…" She gave her embroidery a good jab.

Julia nudged her with her elbow. "Well, go on. Tell all."

Her gaze went off into the middle distance. "Dameron Carlisle. He wasn't tall, but then neither am I. He didn't have a prepossessing build, but I never thought a gentleman needed one. But he had blue eyes you could swim in and the sweetest smile. And he would listen to whatever I had to say for hours."

"He sounds quite perfect," Julia said. "Whyever didn't you marry him?"

Daring tied off a knot. "My father didn't think he was good enough. His family was not well off, you see, though he had a job as a clerk at a prominent London bank. Father refused to consider his suit, and I refused to go against Father's wishes. In the end, I married Mr. Daring, who was quite a few years my senior."

Now Julia sighed. "It sounds very much like my situation."

"Which is why you must know that I speak from experience. If I had stood my ground, insisted on accepting Dameron's proposal, who knows what might have happened? Not that I entirely regretted my marriage. It taught me much. Then again, if I had married Dameron, I would not be sitting beside you now, dispensing advice like a cup of tea."

Julia patted her shoulder. "Well, I am glad you are here now, even if I'm sad you didn't marry your sweetheart. I won't forget the story. I will stand firm."

"So long as the gentleman is worth the effort, dear," she cautioned.

Julia nodded. But she couldn't understand why the gentleman that popped into her mind wasn't Lord Westerbrook but Tanner.

Tanner was still smiling when he knocked at the door of Mr. Hewett's study. Julia might lose her temper easily, but she certainly gave as good as she got. He could only hope her viscount appreciated the fact.

He schooled his face as his employer called for him to enter. Hewett was sitting at his desk, hands clasped over his belly. At the sight of Tanner, his own smile turned up.

"Ah, the man of the hour. Did she blister your ears for throwing the jackanapes out?"

"She only warmed them," Tanner assured him, moving into the room.

Hewett motioned him into the chair in front of his desk. "And what did you think of the fellow?"

Nothing that would endear the fellow to Julia's father. "I only had a few moments with him."

"But I wager you generally take a man's measure in as short a time," Hewett said. "Am I wrong to be warning Julia away from him?"

This was his opportunity to help Julia's father see the man she loved was the right man for her. He ought to extoll Lord Westerbrook's insights, his character. At the very least his golden good looks. He couldn't make himself do it.

"No need to warn," he allowed. "But it is never a bad idea to become better acquainted before agreeing to a lasting union."

Hewett eyed him. "So you'll say nothing against the fellow."

Tanner shrugged. "He seemed surer of himself than his consequence might warrant."

Hewett slapped his hands down on the arms of his chair. "And if that isn't a good way of saying he's conceited, I don't know what is. What I can't understand is why Julia doesn't see it. She has a good head on her shoulders, her temper notwithstanding."

"There's no accounting for taste," Tanner said, though he'd wondered as much. There was something manipulative about the viscount, as if he saw others as things to use for his purposes. Julia Hewett could do better.

Her father leaned forward. "But you didn't come to talk about Westerbrook, did you? Is something else afoot?"

"Not with your daughter," Tanner told him. "But

she confided that she heard part of a conversation this afternoon that troubled her. Another man apparently threatened you."

Hewett waved a hand. "That was nothing. Jacobs is a squeaky little fellow afraid of his own shadow. He might bluster, but he won't back up the sound with action."

"You've crossed him before, then," Tanner surmised.

"Not really. He's invested in a string of canals between here and Runnymeade. I invested too, but that didn't stop me from investing in the railway as well. Now that the railway is about to launch, he thinks I cheated him. Tell Julia there's no need for concern."

"Concern is my job," Tanner said. "Would you like me to look into him?"

Hewett leaned back. "That might not be a bad idea, now that you mention it. Make sure the little pug doesn't have a bite to match his bark. By all means, so long as you don't leave Julia unprotected. See what you can discover about Rufus Jacobs. He lives near Weybridge."

Tanner rose and clapped a fist to his chest. "Your servant, sir."

Hewett nodded, and Tanner left him.

Here, at last, was something worth doing. He could take one of Hewett's prize mounts, ride over to Weybridge, and ask a few questions about this Jacobs. Movement, action. Perhaps a tiny bit of adventure.

And how exactly could he do that and remain on guard with Julia?

CHAPTER SEVEN

IN THE END, Tanner decided to give the task to Keller. He couldn't very well justify galloping all over the county after a danger that might be no danger after all. He went to his room, where Pepin was pressing one of his coats. The lad was happy to find him writing materials instead.

Tanner jotted off a note to Keller and handed it to his valet. "Can you locate someone to deliver this to Rose Hill at their earliest convenience?"

Pepin's head bobbed. "Yes, sir. Right away, sir."

He consoled himself with the fact that he'd given his friend something to do while Keller looked for his own position.

Preferably one more challenging than this one.

At times, when King Frederick and his sons had first been exiled from Batavaria, the Imperial Guards had had to be constantly on the alert. Württemberg, the kingdom that had subsumed their country, was determined to keep it. He'd foiled assassination attempts in ballrooms among the German states and vineyards in the hills of Italy. He should be grateful that here, the most he found were overweening viscounts and veiled threats.

The next day, Julia was planning to determine where to stage the balloon ascension. With lawns stretching in every direction, he would have thought it an easy task, but apparently more was involved. She and Daring holed up in the library, checking maps and jotting notes. Until they left or someone called, they had no need of him.

He'd go mad sitting about. He grabbed his weapons and took them to the kitchen garden beside the house to practice.

Whoever had been leading the Imperial Guard had run them through drills every day. Roth had continued the practice when the four of them had decided to stay in England. Tanner started with the sword. He'd seen English gentlemen strip out of coats to drill, but such coats were tailored to show off their physiques.

"Ours must have enough room to move," Huber had told the tailor they'd used in London.

"A villain will hardly wait while we request a moment to remove our coats," Tanner had explained to the goggle-eyed tailor.

Now, the coat felt good against the cool autumn air as he practiced the movements. Elbow up and block, elbow down and lunge. To the right, to the left. It was more effective if he had a partner, but this would have to do. Still, he was obviously out of practice. He could feel the sweat dampening his back.

"Harder!" His father's voice rang in his mind. "If you wish to be an Imperial Guard, you must be able to beat any man in a fair fight."

Cocky even then, he'd grinned. "Why must it be fair?"

His father's grin was bigger. "That's my boy."

His boy. The son of Kristof Tanner the first. Destined for greatness.

Even if it killed him.

He sheathed the sword and set it aside. In the end, it hadn't been misplaced bravado that had killed his father but a sudden seizure of the heart. Still Tanner had been unable to step out from under the shadow. Trying to match or best his father's legend had nearly gotten him killed. But he had survived the orphan school where he'd been trained as a soldier, the many battles with the French, the palace intrigue, and the years of exile. And he had done the one thing his father never had: travel. If he found the right man to guard, he might go further yet. Beyond the narrow horizon into glory.

He shook himself and fisted his hands. Perhaps some practice with boxing, though that was even more difficult with no opponent. Fortunately, Sir Matthew Bateman, who had been a noted pugilist before his elevation, had taught the four of them some tactics while they had been guarding his sister. Tanner jabbed, throwing his weight behind the movement. Left, left, right, right. Repeat. He did squats and jumps. Now he could feel the dampness behind his legs as well.

Finally, he pulled the two knives from his boots and hurled them into a post that had apparently been used to string beans, if the browning vines curling around it were any indication. He walked the short distance, retrieved the blades, and backed up a little more. The first knife embedded itself just enough to stand quivering. Sloppy.

A noise behind him had him whirling, remaining knife up and at the ready.

Mrs. Daring blinked, and Julia raised her brows.

"We were about to walk the lawns," she explained. "Garrison indicated you were out here, so we came to find you. What has the post done that you feel the need to skewer it repeatedly?"

He smiled, lowering his arm. "It is a fine post, the right height and width to provide a little challenge." He flipped the knife over and offered her the hilt. "Care to try?"

Julia had watched Tanner practicing for a few moments before he had noticed. There was a quickness, a grace to his movements, like a deer bounding across the lawns. She had been invited to view a fencing demonstration while in London, and she'd seen Mr. Rowlandson's drawing of the interior of Angelo's Fencing Academy. This seemed more real.

More lethal.

She eyed the knife he offered her. "You might not like where that lands."

He chuckled. "I've learned to duck and dodge over the years. I'll take my chances."

"There is something to be said for a gentleman who knows his limitations," Daring offered, but she stepped to one side, as if to be out of the way of any mistakes.

Julia accepted the knife. It was about six inches long, sharply tailored to a point, with a hilt made of some kind of horn marked with a picture of a stag.

"Did you carve the hilt yourself?" she asked him, admiring the design.

"No," he said, "but the pattern is rough enough that I can grip the hilt even when I'm wearing evening gloves. A Batavarian trick."

"Very wise," she said. "And you just throw it?" She curled back her arm and attempted to hurl the knife down the row of beans as she'd seen him just do. The blade barely managed a few feet before plummeting into the dirt.

"Perhaps a little harder," he suggested. He went to retrieve it and the one sticking out of the post. Returning to her side, he set one of the blades on the stone lip of the garden bed and positioned himself behind her.

"Hold it like this," he said. His arm ran alongside hers, sleeve against sleeve, fingers brushing hers. A shiver went through her as he slipped the hilt into her grip and turned her fingers around the horn.

With him standing so close it was a wonder she could hold anything at all! She raised her chin and gripped the knife.

"Feel the difference?" he asked, voice a purr in her ear.

"Yes," she said, entirely too breathlessly. She was beginning to sound like her companion! "It's balanced in the middle."

"The best knives are," Daring informed her from the safety of the next row over.

"Indeed," Tanner agreed. "Now, imagine that post is your worst enemy."

"I don't have enemies, sir," Julia informed him primly.

"Certainly none that throw knives, thank the good Lord," Daring said.

"Then pretend you have a great distaste for that post," Tanner suggested.

She laughed, but she focused on the target. "I am prepared to assault the poor post."

"Excellent." Cool air brushed her as he stepped back and around to her other side. "Raise your whole arm with the knife until your elbow is above your chest bone and the hilt is aligned with your ear."

"As if I were brushing the back of my hair," she said, doing as he bid.

"Perhaps not quite so far. There!"

She held the knife poised.

"Now, as you take a step, bring your arm down and straighten it, releasing the knife. Your fingers should point toward your target."

She drew in a breath, yanked down her arm, and released the knife. It flew along the row, clattered against the post, and fell to the ground.

Julia shook her head.

"A good try," he allowed, turning to smile at her.

"There is obviously a skill to it," she said. "Perhaps I will leave it to you. Apparently I lack the desire to skewer inanimate wooden objects."

"Mastering any skill requires practice," Daring reminded her, rejoining them.

Julia made a face. "And that is the one thing I abhor: the

practicing." She smiled at Tanner. "Shall we go find the perfect spot for Lady Worthington's balloon ascension?"

"Of course." He turned to where he'd left the other knife and frowned. The lip of the bed lay empty.

Julia joined him in glancing around. It took her a moment to sight the second knife embedded in the post. Odd. She hadn't remembered him throwing. He went to retrieve his knife, then, to her astonishment, tucked one in each of his boots.

"Do you always walk around like that?" she asked.

"When I cannot carry my sword and pistol easily," he admitted. "And when a little extra protection might be necessary."

"I pity any post we might meet," she assured him.

He laughed.

And so they set off across the rear lawns. She and Daring had discussed angles for viewing and flat areas for the ascension. As Julia had suspected, the slope from the house to the lake did not seem like much, but it was entirely unsuited to a balloon launch. And it lacked some of the characteristics Lady Worthington had requested.

"We need a level pad approximately twenty feet square," she'd written, "with no trees within forty feet and no brush or shrubbery within ten. For our water landing experiment, we also need a body of still water at least thirty feet on the longer side and twenty on the shorter. I have been told your estate offers the ideal situation, and I am delighted you are willing to accommodate us."

Julia wasn't sure who had told the noted natural philosophers about her father's estate, but she was determined to give them exactly what they requested. Accordingly, she led Tanner down toward the lake, Daring strolling along on his other side.

"Was this natural?" he asked as they reached the rushes at one end.

"There was a pond," Julia said. "The gentleman who

designed our landscape broadened and deepened it. I understand it's fed by an underground spring. It can get a bit low in the late summer, but the autumn rains have already helped to replenish it."

Indeed, the still waters reflected the clouds above, making it appear as if lengths of cotton floated on the blue. It was certainly long enough and wide enough to suit Lady Worthington's landing, but where to start?

"This reminds me of the pond near where I grew up," he said, though his gaze kept sweeping the area as if he were sure danger lurked in the tall grasses on the other side.

"You lived in the country, then," she said.

He sent her a smile. "No. I was born in the capital, within a short walk of the king's castle. There was an ornamental pond in our part of the city. It froze in winter, and we'd skate on it."

Julia beamed. "Oh, that sounds delightful! I love to ice skate."

"She flies across the ice," Daring said. "But then, she flies about most places in one form or another."

Julia turned her gaze to the lake. "So far, it hasn't frozen hard enough to ice this up, though Lady Belfort's pond at Rose Hill is generally frozen over before Christmas. Her family has hosted a Christmas Eve party with skating for decades."

"And plenty of gingerbread," Daring put in with a longing sigh.

"Perhaps I will have an opportunity to take part," he mused. "Though I suspect you will not be in need of a bodyguard by then."

Did he mean because she would be married to Westie? Her spirits rose at the thought. "I sincerely hope you're right. But you never know. Even as Lady Westerbrook, I might require extra protection. I've always wanted to travel. India, the Ottoman Empire, the Americas! How wonderful to see more than Surrey and London, to learn more, to experience other cultures."

He glanced her way. "And Lord Westerbrook, he shares these dreams?"

Julia put a hand to her bonnet as the breeze came up, ruffling the waters of the lake and turning the reflections into strips of white. "Perhaps not yet, and of course he has his duty to Parliament and his tenants. But I'm hoping to convince him to make at least one trip every few years." She glanced his way. "You've traveled with your king, I understand. Where would you suggest we start?"

He stuck out his lower lip as if giving the matter thought. "The Continent, perhaps. It's closer to hand, and the cultures are not so different as here. Once Lord Westerbrook is accustomed to traveling, you can try something more adventurous. I have read of the monuments in Egypt. Stone sphinxes hundreds of times the size of a man, pyramids that reach the sky, and all more ancient than anything we might find here."

She could imagine it too, the sun warming her, the sky clear and blue and stretching forever. "That sounds marvelous. When do we leave?"

She was teasing. He could see it in her smile and the sparkle in her eyes.

"You have a companion," he told her. "You have reached your majority. Go tomorrow."

Mrs. Daring sniffed. "Nonsense. It would take me a fortnight to make the arrangements and at least a day to pack."

Julia laughed. "Don't worry, Daring. I'm not planning to leave anytime soon. Father would never allow it."

She turned her attention to the grounds around the lake, and clouds covered the sun. He was sorry to see her light dim as well. Her enthusiasm stoked his. But she was right that two women alone could find traveling dangerous at the best of times. Better to wait until she had a husband and faithful retainers to accompany her.

"There," she said, pointing to an area of grass on the other side of the lake. "It has the dimensions and aspects Lady Worthington requested. If that's where we set up the balloon, we can have the crowd here, on the slope. That way, everyone should have a good view."

"Excellent choice," Mrs. Daring said. "Shall we return to the house for tea?"

Tanner prepared himself for another stultifying afternoon. Perhaps he could find a good book in the library.

Garrison was waiting as they came back through the house.

"Your father asked me to inform you that we will have company for dinner this evening, Miss Hewett," he said as he took her pelisse. A footman attended to Mrs. Daring. Neither of the men bothered with Tanner.

"Oh?" she asked. "One of Father's investors?"

"That I could not say," Garrison replied as the footman took away the garments. "Your father asked that you be down at half-past five." Finally he glanced at Tanner. "You are to join them."

So far, Mr. Hewett had had him eat with them at the table for dinner every night. Did the pointed invitation suggest there was something dangerous about this visitor?

"When will Mr. Hewett's guest arrive?" Tanner asked.

"I do not inquire as to the master's business," Garrison said, narrowing his eyes. He could look as stern as Roth when he tried.

Tanner thought to remain in the entry hall, if only to annoy the butler, but Julia decided to take a ride before dinner, and so he went with her and Mrs. Daring along the trees edging the estate. As her father had bragged, she was a bruising rider. Tanner was just surprised that Mrs.

Daring matched her, even when Julia and Tanner raced back to the stables.

And so it wasn't until he came down to dinner with the pair that he found an older man seated at his employer's left. They both stood as the ladies entered.

"Look who dropped by," her father said with a nod toward the other gentleman. "Julia, my dear, Mrs. Daring, allow me to present Harold, Marquess of Norfall. Norfall, this is my girl, Julia, and her companion. And that strapping fellow is her bodyguard, Mr. Tanner, formerly of the Batavarian Imperial Guard."

So, his employer hadn't mentioned Tanner and Julia's pretend engagement to the fellow.

The marquess inclined his head. An older man with the nose of a horse and the jowls of a bulldog, he seemed to fill his evening coat with more muscle than Tanner would have thought possible. Padding, perhaps?

"Miss Hewett, Mrs. Daring, a pleasure," the marquess said in a nasally voice. "Mr. Tanner, I had the honor of meeting your king. Fine fellow. Very glad to hear his kingdom was returned to him."

Tanner clapped his fist to his chest. "My lord. Thank you."

They were all seated, Julia next to her father on the right with Daring beside her. Tanner took up his place next to the marquess, where he could see Julia, the room at large, and the two doors.

"Norfall has invested in my railroad," Hewett explained after the grace had been said and the dinner of pork roast, Yorkshire pudding, and pumpkin preserves had been served by footmen in white powdered wigs and black tailcoats.

"Best to keep up with these advancements, I believe," the marquess said. "My late wife used to read *Philosophical Transactions* to me in the evening."

Hewett barked a laugh as he tucked into his roast. "Oh, that should put you straight to sleep."

"Not at all," the marquess assured him. "I found it fascinating." He looked to Julia. "What do you prefer to read, Miss Hewett? I understand the younger set greatly enjoys gothic novels, ruined castles, ghostly apparitions, that sort of thing."

"I am quite partial to *Sense and Sensibility* and *Pride and Prejudice*," she said. "But I would not turn up my nose at a Scotch novel."

He did turn up his long nose. "Romantic claptrap, if you ask me. The Scots are only one generation removed from barbarism."

Julia choked on her pumpkin. "The noted poet Robert Burns might take exception to that remark," she managed after swallowing. "What do you enjoy reading, Tanner, dear?"

CHAPTER EIGHT

O H, BUT SHE was in rare form. Tanner tried not to smile, but the marquess blinked as if he'd misheard her, and her father glowered at her.

"I have tried your Scotch novels recently," Tanner answered her. "Great adventures. Jonathan Swift holds similar appeal."

"*Gulliver's Travels.*" She grinned at him. "One of my favorites as well. I'm so glad to hear my betrothed enjoys the same sort of literature."

The marquess frowned. "Betrothed?"

"Bodyguard," her father insisted with another look to her. "Much too soon to be talking of betrothals. More roast, Norfall?" He nodded to the footman, who dutifully trotted forward to offer the platter.

They talked about many things over the meal. Tanner mostly listened. He was more interested in behavior. The marquess made sure to bring Julia into any conversation her father started. Indeed, he kept his gaze on her, at times pensive, at times almost disappointed.

Julia, meanwhile, argued any point she found ridiculous or offensive, her own countenance darkening as the evening wore on. Though she and Daring usually left the table at the same time as her father, she rose before the dessert course had finished.

"I'm sure you gentlemen have many business matters to discuss. We'll leave you to it. Come, Daring."

Her companion sighed, but she suffered herself to follow her from the room.

Tanner rose as well.

"So, what do you think?" Hewett asked his guest as Tanner headed for the door. "Pretty, cultured, intelligent, just as I said."

"You have raised her well," the marquess replied. "But I remain unsure that she is the sort I would want in my second wife."

Tanner nearly stumbled but managed to quit the room without letting on he'd heard. Was he slipping that he hadn't realized what was happening? So much for Julia's hope that their engagement would prevent her father from matchmaking.

She evidently had caught the drift. She was pacing the upstairs withdrawing room while Daring sat on the sofa, head turning as she watched.

Julia stopped to look at Tanner as he entered. "And you couldn't throw *him* out?"

He spread his hands. "He is no danger to you. And he wasn't trying to kiss your hand."

"No, merely chain himself to me." She shuddered. "Scots are barbarians indeed."

"One generation away," Tanner corrected her.

She threw up her hands. "As if that's any better. And did you hear his opinions on literature for ladies? I begin to think *he's* the barbarian."

She made sure to retire before her father and his guest could join them.

Tanner ought to retire as well, but part of him wanted to know whether the savvy businessman had convinced the marquess to marry his daughter. Accordingly, he was in the withdrawing room when the two gentlemen entered.

Her father glanced around, frown growing. "Where's Julia?"

"Miss Hewett pleaded a headache," Tanner said. "She and Mrs. Daring have retired for the evening."

"Just as well," the marquess said. "I should start for home. It's a short distance to my estate at Burhill, but the light fades quickly these days. If you'd be so good as to call for my carriage."

Hewett's face reddened, but he looked to Garrison, who had also come in, and his butler moved to do as the marquess wished.

"You," his employer said, pointing at Tanner, "stay here. I'd like a word."

He waited only until the marquess had been escorted to the door before rounding on Tanner. "You didn't have to help her."

"I didn't help her," Tanner said. "I never claimed we were betrothed in front of your guest. I didn't give her a headache."

"You could have insisted she stay."

"You pay me to protect her. Nothing more."

Hewett's eyes narrowed. "You didn't care for him either, I take it. I'll have you know he's worth a pretty penny. He has a fine estate here in Surrey, a cottage in the Lakes District, and a townhouse in London, and his name is as old as the Conquest."

"He is also a great deal older than your daughter and shares few of her views, even on something as benign as literature," Tanner pointed out. "Do you think she would be happy with him?"

Hewett sighed as he dropped onto the sofa. "Perhaps not. So that's what she wants, eh? A young upstart who likes adventure novels?"

Having been given no leave to sit as well, Tanner remained standing. "She is your daughter. I would be impertinent to tell you what she wants."

Hewett glanced up at him. "But I wager she's told you."

Would he be betraying a confidence? Or helping Julia

achieve her dreams? He decided to take a chance. "She said only that she wants a husband who will love and honor her, one she can love and honor in return."

"You can't eat love," her father said with a shake of his head. "And honor will only take you so far. Still, they aren't bad characteristics. I'm just not sure her viscount has them."

Neither was Tanner. But, come what may, the choice was Julia's and Julia's alone. She wasn't a princess whose marriage would secure an alliance. As the daughter of an entrepreneur, she could marry who she liked. He would do what he could to protect her choice.

Julia made sure to be at the breakfast table in time to catch her father the next morning. He was seated at the head of the small table in the sunny room with its south-facing windows overlooking the lake, stirring sugar into his coffee.

"No," she said, taking her seat beside him as Daring sat opposite her.

He frowned. "I don't recall asking your opinion."

"You may be able to drag me to the altar," she said. "But you can't make me speak my vows. That's still a requirement for marriage, as far as I know."

"Rotten shame," he muttered. "But point taken. You didn't care for the wisdom and wealth of the marquess."

Julia nodded her thanks to the footman, who had set a cup of chocolate in front of her. "The marquess had little wisdom, Father, and I have entirely enough wealth, thank you very much."

He pointed his teaspoon at her, dripping coffee on the pristine white tablecloth. "Yes, you should be thanking me. And I'll thank you not to waste my hard work on some fellow who doesn't deserve it."

"And I will thank you not to engage me to someone else after you told everyone I was engaged to Tanner. Our friends and neighbors will think me fast."

Her father waved away the platter of eggs the footman offered. "Give them to my daughter. I've lost my appetite." He tossed down his napkin and quit the room.

Julia sighed. Perhaps she shouldn't have been so hard on him. He was only trying to make sure she had a secure future. He simply didn't understand that she wanted more.

Tanner came in then, and the footman hastily served him, earning her servant a word of thanks. "And what do we have planned today?" Tanner asked.

He sounded as enthused as if he expected she was going to spend the day scrubbing floors.

"Nothing onerous," she assured him. "I am meeting with the staff this morning to give them the final plans for the ascension."

"Lord and Lady Worthington will arrive late this afternoon," Daring put in.

"And before then," Julia continued, "Daring and I will be going over our winter wardrobes to see what else needs to be purchased for this year."

"Gloves and boots wear out so quickly here," Daring said with a sigh.

"Delightful," Tanner said. The word sounded anything but. He took a long pull of the coffee the footman had poured him, as if he needed its support.

"You could toss pointy things at the posts in the garden," Julia suggested.

"Or perhaps Pepin would appreciate tutelage in the military arts," Daring added.

His eyes lit at that. "Excellent idea, Mrs. Daring. Send word if you need me."

She did not anticipate any possible danger that day,

so she merely nodded. But she had only finished her meeting with the staff when one of the footmen came to tell her that she had a caller.

"Miss Bee," he said, voice catching on the name.

Her stomach clenched. "The elder?" she clarified. "Not the mother and both daughters?"

"Just the one, miss, and her maid, who I took the liberty of inviting down to the servant's hall. Her coachman is being taken care of at the stables."

"Very kind of you all," she said. "I suppose I'll go see what she wants."

Drawing a breath as if in fortification, Daring followed her out.

Miss Bee was standing in the formal withdrawing room, tugging at a recalcitrant blond curl as she regarded herself in the mirror with a troubled frown. She hastily put on a smile and turned as Julia and Daring entered.

"Miss Hewett, thank you so much for receiving me," she said.

"You are very welcome," Julia said, nodding toward the sofa. "Won't you have a seat?"

Miss Bee sank onto the horsehair sofa. Daring took up a spot at the very corner and folded her hands into her lap. Julia took the closest chair.

"How might I help you?" Julia asked.

Miss Bee's golden lashes fluttered. "Oh, I wasn't seeking help. Not precisely. I simply noticed you find it uncomfortable when Mother and Angelica and I all visit at once. We can be overwhelming, I've been told. I thought perhaps it would be easier for you if it was just me."

Rather kind of her, even if she mistook Julia's reasoning. She had never felt overwhelmed by crowds.

"And how are your mother and sister?" she asked dutifully. She should probably offer refreshments, but she simply could not find it in herself to encourage a lengthy visit.

"Well, thank you," her guest replied. "Greatly looking forward to the balloon ascension tomorrow. Will you be going up?"

"I would love to," Julia told her. "But Lady Worthington and her husband are conducting an experiment, as I mentioned. We are merely privileged to watch."

"Oh, of course. I told Mother as much, but she insisted that if it were her estate, she'd make sure she had a chance to ride along."

Very likely she would. "Well, be sure to give her my regards," Julia said.

Another lady might have taken the cue to end their interview. Miss Bee merely smiled at her. Of the three, she had the softest lines to her face, and her pale eyes were more clear and earnest. "You can be sure I will. She thinks very highly of you, you know. 'If only you behaved more like Miss Hewett,' she'll tell me, 'think what you might achieve.'"

"I'm sure you'll achieve just fine on your own," Julia said.

If her mother had been in the room, she would have been quick to catalog her daughter's accomplishments. Miss Bee dropped her gaze to her hands, resting in the lap of her lilac-colored kerseymere gown. "That is sweet of you to say, but I have not managed to achieve much thus far. I have middling skill at the piano, you would not wish to hear me sing more than a chorus, and my embroidery ends up in terrible knots no matter how hard I try. But I do love to dance."

She had not thought to find anything in common. "So do I," Julia confided. "And I've noticed you make a good showing at the assemblies."

"Aren't they the most fun?" Her smile raised Julia's spirits as well. "You will be coming to the one later this month? I hear the committee hired a quartet from London to play. They are sure to know the latest music and dances."

"Oh, that will be delightful! Now, if we can just find enough gentlemen to fill the dancefloor!"

She made a face. "Things have certainly been thin there. But of course we will have Mr. Tanner and Mr. Keller of the Batavarian Imperial Guard. They are both very light on their feet."

"Indeed they are. I'm sure I can arrange for Mr. Tanner to partner you."

"Oh, how lovely." Once more her gaze fell. "Though it is possible I may have to attend with my fiancé."

Julia cocked her head. "I had not heard you were engaged. Congratulations."

"I'm not engaged as yet," she allowed. "Mother is determined that I wed a titled gentleman, and Father has been inviting them to call. The Marquess of Norfall was by the other day."

She and Julia shuddered together. So, Julia wasn't the only one to be considered by the elderly marquess. Was he hunting an heiress? Miss Bee's fortune was rumored to be only slightly less than her own.

"You will have to live with the fellow your entire life," she told her visitor. "He must be up to your standards, not your mother and father's."

Her smile was sad. "I quite agree, but I have found it challenging to stand up to my mother. You may have noticed she is a force of nature."

"As is my father," Julia assured her. She reached out and took one of Miss Bee's hands. "But if we stand together, they must both fall back."

"Do you truly think so?" Her voice held such hope.

"Absolutely," Julia said. "They may find we are forces of nature as well. Please, Miss Bee, call me Julia, and I will call you Elspeth. Feel free to visit any time."

Pepin was indeed delighted to learn anything Tanner wanted to teach him, so the two spent a pleasant hour going through fencing drills in the kitchen garden, out of sight of most of the house. The lad's arms could use a few more muscles, but he acquitted himself well.

"Better than I did my first time," Tanner assured him as they finished. "My father nearly ran me through."

Pepin's eyes widened. "Your own father?"

"He had high expectations of his only son," Tanner explained as they moved toward the kitchen. "For me, it was more about the thrill of winning. You should have seen his face the first time I beat him."

Pepin grinned. "So you always wanted to be like your father."

"Perhaps a little," Tanner admitted. "Though I've always wanted to see more of the world."

He handed the lad his sword, and Pepin scurried off to stow the blades. Mrs. Cheevers glanced up as Tanner crossed the kitchen.

"Well, there you are! I thought you'd be upstairs with the ladies and their visitor."

Tanner stopped to regard her. "Miss Hewett has a visitor?"

Perhaps his tone was harsher than he intended, for the cook blushed. "One of the Bees, I think the elder daughter. Her maid was just taking tea in the servant's hall."

Miss Bee the elder likely wasn't a danger, but he was still Julia's bodyguard. He nodded his thanks and strode from the room.

The formal withdrawing room was empty, as was the library. Julia would not have entertained a visitor in her father's study. Tanner climbed the stairs, checked the upper withdrawing room, then rapped on her bedchamber door.

"Come," she called.

He stepped inside to find a pretty sitting room done in shades of blue with white curlicues on the ceiling and along the tops of the walls, like icing on a cake. Julia and Mrs. Daring had pelisses, cloaks, muffs, and gloves spread out over the two chairs by the fire, the chaise longue near the window, and the side tables here and there. Inventory had begun.

"Oh, Tanner, it's you," she said, fringed shawl up in her arms. "Are all the posts safe?"

"I understand you had a visitor," he said.

A frown began to gather. "Yes. Is that a problem?"

He blew out a breath before moving closer. "I am to be on duty whenever there are strangers in the house. If I am not alerted, I cannot protect you. Unless, of course, you would prefer that I follow you about all day like a lap dog."

Mrs. Daring's hands began fluttering.

"Certainly not," Julia said with a sniff. "But it was just Miss Bee the elder. I wasn't in any danger."

He raised a brow. "You seemed to think any of the Bees sufficiently dangerous that you must escape them last time they called."

She smiled as if she remembered as well. "It was all of them last time. Just one turned out to be rather pleasant."

"Refreshingly so," Mrs. Daring agreed. "Though I'm not sure I'd say the same for her mother and younger sister."

"Indeed," Julia said. "As it is, I find myself quite in charity with Elspeth."

So they had decided to call each other by their first names. That said something here in England.

"I'm sorry I didn't think to call you," she continued.

"As you can see, we are reviewing our wardrobes. You are welcome to join us."

"I'm sure that would be fascinating," he said.

She raised her chin. "I know sarcasm when I hear it, sir. It might behoove you to understand what sorts of items a lady needs for a winter in Surrey. You don't know where you will be assigned next."

"Preferably not protecting a lady in Surrey in winter," he said. "I spent enough winters in Batavaria as it is. Now, along the southern Italian coast, that's a lovely place to spend the winter."

And, for some reason, he could picture her there beside him, strolling the sunlit beaches, parasol twirling. She'd turn and smile, and he'd bend closer…

"So," Tanner said, straightening. "What does a lady need in winter?"

Because going through coats and gloves was much safer than dreaming of what could never be.

CHAPTER NINE

FORTUNATELY, TANNER WAS spared an afternoon looking over shawls and pelisses and fur-lined gloves by having to meet with a caller of his own. Pepin came to tell him that Keller was here to speak with him. Of course, Garrison had sent Tanner's friend round to the servant's entrance.

Tanner met him in the kitchen. Mrs. Cheevers and her assistants were already cooing over his friend, the cook offering a Bath bun fresh from the oven, and her pot girl bringing him tea and nearly sloshing it on herself in her haste.

"Thank you for being so kind to my friend," Tanner told them all. "But I would expect no less from the sterling ladies of this kitchen."

They all blushed.

"You may use the servant's hall if you desire a private word, sirs," Mrs. Cheevers said with a nod down the corridor. "Most everyone else is upstairs preparing for dinner."

Keller thanked them for their trouble, picked up his goodies, then headed with Tanner for the servant's hall. It had white-washed walls and windows looking out onto the rear yard. Four doors to what were likely storage rooms made a row of brown across the back.

Tanner took a seat at the long table in the center of the room. "What's happened?"

Keller hurriedly swallowed his bite of bun as he straddled the bench beside him. "You asked me to look into Mr. Jacobs, the canal owner. I thought you would want to hear what I learned."

Setting down his tea, he pulled a small notebook from the pocket of his navy coat and flipped it open. "Following the information you provided, I rode south and asked a few questions of various people."

Keller had always been good at such studies. Like the ladies in the kitchen, most were glad to make his acquaintance.

"And what did these people tell you?" Tanner asked.

Keller considered his notes. "Mr. Jacobs resides a few miles to the southwest of Weybridge, near one of his own canals. The stone house is quite a bit smaller than this one or Rose Hill, but larger than our cottage there. His stable hands say he is stingy with his wages and rewards."

"Most stable hands would say the same," Tanner said with a chuckle.

Keller glanced up with a grin. "Most bodyguards too." He turned the page in his notebook. "He has invested in a number of canals. Some appear to be doing well. The ones closer to the new railway are struggling."

Tanner set his elbow on the table and leaned his chin on his palm. "So, he does have a grievance against Mr. Hewett in that area."

"No more so than anyone else in his situation. But I do not think he will be coming for Mr. Hewett any time soon." He shut his notebook and met Tanner's gaze, his blue eyes turning down. "He was robbed by highwaymen yesterday. He attempted to argue with them and was struck for his trouble. He is lying unconscious at home. The physician is hopeful he will eventually recover."

Tanner dropped his arm. "Highwaymen? There was talk last month, but I thought His Grace, the Duke of Wey, had seen to their capture."

"He tried," Keller said, voice turning grim. "He is serving as magistrate only until one can be appointed, and he has many more matters to attend to. When no more coaches were robbed, he may have thought his vigilance had driven the villains from the area. I don't know if these are the same ones, of course, but they seem to know something about their victims, and they appear to be ruthless."

He could only be glad Julia didn't have any plans to travel about the area any farther than Rose Hill. Then another thought intruded. "You said they seem to know about their victims. Why?"

"According to Jacobs' coachman, they asked for him by name, and they knew he was carrying a certain sum of gold. They only attacked when he attempted to offer less."

Tanner nodded. "They might have been associated with him, or they may be studying the area, like us."

"Then anyone with any standing could be in danger," Keller said. "The duke, the Marquess of Kendall."

"These highwaymen would be fools to accost an aristocrat," Tanner said. "Besides, we both know dukes and marquesses rarely carry money with them. They have staff make such arrangements. No, I'd be more concerned for Mr. Hewett."

Keller paled. "And the Bees."

Tanner met his gaze. "Even worse, can you think of anything better than a gathering of wealthy citizens at a balloon ascension?"

Keller's fair brows rose. "Lady Belfort plans to attend too. It's a good thing Roth will be joining her. It appears we may be needed."

Lord and Lady Worthington and their cavalcade arrived that afternoon, as planned. The natural philosophers and their two assistants came in one carriage, their various equipment in the two wagons following. Julia, Daring, and Tanner, with Garrison and the footmen flanking, met them on the drive.

"Welcome, welcome," Julia said as they stepped down from the carriage. "You cannot know how delighted we are to host you and your marvelous craft."

She had met the Worthingtons in London at a talk sponsored by the Royal Society. Lady Worthington's petite figure and wide eyes had made her seem out of place among so many darkly dressed, serious-minded gentlemen. Today, she was gowned in the height of fashion in an apple red promenade dress tucked to emphasize her figure and trimmed with braided scallops of the same material. Her pretty face was framed by a lace-edged cap, covered by a chocolate-colored, wide-brimmed velvet hat with red satin ribbons. She quite put Julia's favorite Pomona green pelisse and peacock-feathered bonnet in the shade.

Now she trained vivid green eyes to the shaped wicker basket sticking up from one of the wagons. "She is rather a marvel, isn't she? It's still a thrill every time we take her up."

Her husband seemed to have lost his top hat, for the breeze ruffled his hair, a shade of red between Julia's and Tanner's, as he took his wife's hand and brought it to his lips for a kiss. "I maintain it is the company more than the flight that provides the thrill."

She blushed happily.

Envy grumbled, but Julia silenced it. Perhaps someday, she and Westie would stand before those pyramids Tanner had mentioned, and he would gaze at her with such a besotted look. Until then, she had a duty and a privilege. Her father might have sequestered himself in his study, but she was his hostess.

"It's a delight to see you both again," she said. "You

may remember my companion, Mrs. Daring. May I make you known to my betrothed, Mr. Tanner?"

Nods and smiles were exchanged, though she caught Tanner glancing her way, brows up, as if he wondered that she would claim connection in such company.

Lord Worthington narrowed his grey eyes. "Tanner. Were you not a member of the Batavarian contingent?"

Tanner inclined his head. "I was, my lord. Good of you to remember."

Lady Worthington beamed at her husband. "I'm amazed Worth remembers anything with all the knowledge he's gained over the years."

"And I generally leave the social niceties to my wife," he admitted. "But my sister-in-law, Lady Ashforde, sings your praises on occasion."

"Dear Tuny," his wife said with a fond smile. "I never was entirely certain why she required a bodyguard, but apparently it is the done thing, as Meredith tells me that another of your group was protecting her and her companion. Is that how you met?" Her emerald gaze swung from Julia to Tanner.

"Pardon me." Garrison stepped forward before Julia could respond. "There appears to be some confusion as to where we are to put the balloon tonight."

"I thought the stables," Julia said with a look to her guests. "We have room near the carriages."

"I'm afraid we'll be spending much of tonight in inflation," Lord Worthington said.

Lady Worthington made a face. "We have been using hydrogen of late. Neither of us is particularly enamored of the vile stuff, but it keeps its buoyancy longer than hot air."

"Until we develop a way to keep the air hot," her husband muttered, eyes narrowing once more.

"Be that as it may," Lady Worthington said. "If you

would show our assistants to the spot you have chosen for the launch, they can begin the process."

Between Garrison and the footmen on the inside and grooms on the outside, the Worthingtons and their various boxes, bags, and equipment were soon sorted. Julia could not help noticing that Tanner took it upon himself to chat with each of the visitors' staff, his smile friendly and his gaze alert. Making sure of no mischief, perhaps?

"Will you need to attend the inflation process?" Julia asked as she, Lady Worthington, and Daring finally had a moment in the formal withdrawing room. Lord Worthington had insisted on seeing the physical arrangements and was out touring the rear lawns and lake with their groundskeeper.

"Worth and I will take turns," she said. "We try to note times, any difficulties, that sort of thing. Having the information allows us to better gauge our future experiments."

Julia shook her head. "You amaze me. However did you settle on such a course as being a natural philosopher? My father won't hear of anything except me marrying and marrying well."

She wrinkled her pert nose. "Will fathers and brothers never tire of trying to protect us? My brother Beau was determined that I would marry into the aristocracy." She leaned forward and lowered her voice. "We have been members of the gentry since the family began. Apparently our only aim should have been to advance ourselves." She tsked.

"Many do take that aim," Daring said. "And miss."

She trilled a laugh. "Well, I suppose you can say Beau and I finally hit our target. I wanted nothing so much as to be a natural philosopher. Worth and his sister took a chance on me, and Worth and I ended up falling in love. Beau married Lady Lilith, sister to the Earl of Carrolton.

And we're both as happy as can be. But enough about me. I understand you have been quite sought after, Miss Hewett. Do I take it from your questions that you are not fond of your betrothed?"

She could hardly slander Tanner, and, in truth, she was becoming fond of him. Those quick smiles, that wry wit. He at least wasn't afraid to try new things and journey beyond these hallowed shores. She hardly wanted to appear a jilt to this clever woman.

"Tanner and I agreed to a betrothal to please my father," she replied. "I had hoped for a proposal from Lord Westerbrook. Father is not pleased with him."

"Calls him a useless fribble," Daring agreed.

Lady Worthington glanced between them. "Ah. Well, perhaps Lord Westerbrook will do something to distinguish himself." She smiled hopefully.

Her assistant came in just then, and she excused herself to go see to a question about the disposition of the anchoring ropes.

As Lady Worthington was a particular friend of the Belforts, Julia had invited Meredith and Mr. Keller to join them for an early dinner that night. Meredith had been certain Lady Worthington would want to see Fortune as well, as the cat had helped bring her and her husband together. After learning about the inflation process, Julia wasn't sure either of her guests would attend, but Lady Worthington came downstairs in a lovely yellow dinner dress, arm firmly entwined with her husband's in his black evening coat.

Julia, in a gown of deep blue satin, made sure to introduce her father, who immediately began quizzing Lord Worthington about the future of ballooning, and Lady Worthington was soon ensconced on the sofa, crooning to Meredith's pet, who still appeared to be ignoring Julia. It was all she and Daring could do to encourage their guests into the dining room to eat. Fortune deigned to allow Pepin to take her to the kitchen for treats.

But even at the table, her father kept his focus on their titled male guest.

"I understand from Julia that you've been all over the world," he said to Lord Worthington, who was on his right.

His lordship smiled at his wife across the table. "From the Italian Alps to the Moroccan desert."

"Wherever environmental conditions might prove a challenge to our work," her ladyship agreed with an answering smile. "Then again, we have that luxury. But you, Mr. Hewett, are a true innovator, I understand."

Her father chuckled. "Captain of my own ship, as it were."

"And railway," Julia put in from beside Lord Worthington. "It's going to allow all sorts of people to travel."

Tanner, who had seated himself across from her in his usual spot, despite the seating arrangements, sent her a smile. She grinned back.

"It's more for cargo than passengers," her father said. "Industry pays better, for now."

His lordship leaned forward. "And what advancements are you using there, sir?"

"You would have to ask my engineers, my lord," her father answered. "I leave that sort of thing to the experts. But I can tell you that the tracks have been laid from Walton-on-Thames to Lambeth, and we expect the steam engine to make its first run in the next week or so."

Lady Worthington clasped her hands together. "Oh, how exciting! Worth, let's go watch!"

His smile deepened. "My thoughts exactly, my love."

"Right, then," her father declared. "I'll have Julia send an invite when we know the details. We've invited a few others to join us as well. Lady Belfort, I hope we might have the honor of your company."

"Delighted, sir," Meredith said. "And I expect you'll be including Mr. Tanner."

Julia winked at him.

Her father's eyes twinkled. "Wouldn't think of going anywhere without him."

"And Lord Westerbrook?" Lady Worthington asked, turning her smile on Julia.

Her father's happy look faded. "His lordship may be too busy with his wardrobe."

Lady Worthington blinked so rapidly Julia wondered the candles didn't flicker. "A shame."

"Not a shame from where I'm sitting," her father said, digging into the last of his salmon. "Tanner's a far cry better than any lordling I've met."

Julia surged up, forcing the men to their feet as well. "Let's have our dessert in the withdrawing room. Ladies, if you'd join me." She leveled her father with a scowl, then swept out of the room before the men could question her.

"I'm certain Father didn't mean to imply Lord Worthington wasn't, well, worthy," Julia told their guests as they came through the doors between the dining room and the formal withdrawing room.

"I'm certain he didn't," Lady Worthington agreed. "Still, it was a passionate defense of your Mr. Tanner."

"Agreed," Meredith said as Julia motioned to Garrison, who had followed them, to close the doors. "I'm very glad your father is taken with him, Julia, but it is equally clear he has no use for Lord Westerbrook. Is he your choice, then?"

Julia nodded as the four of them took their seats. "I had thought to use this engagement as a way to help Father see that Lord Westerbrook is the right man for me, but he can't if he refuses to spend any time with him!"

The door from the entry hall opened. Pepin peeked in, then ventured in. Fortune wiggled in his arms.

"You can let her down, Pepin," Julia said. "She'll be safe with us."

"Yes, miss." He bent and set the cat on the carpet.

Fortune shook herself, then glanced back at the lad as if offering him her thanks. Pepin smiled at her before backing from the room and shutting the doors.

Fortune turned her gaze on the ladies. Lady Worthington made kissing noises. Julia twitched her skirts in hopes of drawing the cat closer to her instead.

Fortune stalked to Daring and looked up expectantly.

Julia's companion pressed a hand to the bodice of her amethyst gown. "Me? Such an honor."

Fortune jumped up into her lap and made herself comfortable.

Julia reached out a hand, and the cat turned her face away.

"Perhaps you should bring Lord Westerbrook to meet Fortune," Meredith said as Julia slumped in defeat. "Her approval would give you further evidence to present to your father and give you peace of mind as well."

"I don't need peace of mind concerning Lord Westerbrook," Julia promised. "He is perfect."

Meredith squeezed her hand. "Then I am very happy for you. But there are moments when you glance at Mr. Tanner…"

She didn't finish as the door opened, and the gentlemen ambled in. Fortune's head came up, and she slipped down to run to Tanner. Julia found her gaze seeking her bodyguard as well. When had she fallen into that habit? She turned her gaze purposely to Meredith, who smiled a knowing smile.

Still, she had to admit that having Tanner beside her at the ascension the next day was rather gratifying. Lord and Lady Worthington had indeed monitored their inflation, so that at noon, when their avid audience gathered, an apple red and cream striped balloon was straining against its mooring ropes on the other side of the lake. Julia could only wonder if Lady Worthington had chosen her dress to match the balloon or her balloon to match her dress!

Either way, as she had expected, the slope of the lawn provided an excellent vantage point, even on so grey and chill a day that threatened rain. A lively group made up of her friends, her family, and her staff shuffled about the grass, studying the balloon, which was tethered to ropes looped over stakes at each of the four corners of the basket. Tiny Daring even squeezed to the front as if not to miss a moment.

Lord and Lady Worthington had been out since dawn, setting up their equipment and checking it over at least twice. Their excitement was contagious.

"It may look deceptively simple," Lady Worthington had explained to Julia at one point. "But it's actually very hard to control where a balloon lands with any sort of precision. Water landings can be particularly dangerous, hence our experiment."

Now Lord Worthington swung his wife up in his arms to the oohs and aahs of the ladies and deposited her into the wicker basket. A moment later, he used the rigging on either side to haul himself in with her. This time the men cheered. With a happy wave from Lady Worthington, the pair turned to look at the instruments anchored to the basket's gunwale. Julia could see them, nodding, conversing. Then Lady Worthington lifted her arm.

The assistant on the farthest line removed the loop from the stake, then ran to remove the next closest. The basket jerked.

Daring gasped.

Julia stepped closer to Tanner.

The assistant on the opposite loops removed one, and

the balloon strained like a horse ready to be let out to pasture.

Julia caught her breath.

"Now, Thaddeus!" Lady Worthington called to the second assistant.

He yanked off the final rope.

Julia's hand clasped Tanner's and clung as the craft soared toward the sky.

CHAPTER TEN

TANNER GLANCED JULIA'S way in surprise as her fingers found his, but her gaze was latched onto the colorful balloon as its shadow fell over them. He should keep his hands free to protect her, yet the touch of her fingers felt so right. He didn't pull away.

The balloon slowed, then stopped to hover over the lake. Ladies put one hand to their bonnets to gaze upward. More than one top hat tumbled down onto the grass as the men followed suit.

Lord and Lady Worthington's voices came faintly.

"The paddles?"

"Left a little on the pumps. That's right."

"Releasing the gas now."

Something hissed as the balloon dipped gracefully toward the water.

Julia squeezed his hand.

"A little farther," Tanner murmured, watching the water ripple at the balloon's approach. A moment later, and the craft bumped against the lake, then came to rest.

Julia pulled her fingers from his as applause rang out from the observers. But his hand felt oddly empty.

Immediately, two of her grooms set out by rowboat to fetch the Worthingtons, bringing them back to shore to more acclaim. Lady Worthington gathered her skirts and climbed to Julia's side.

"That looked like so much fun!" Julia told her. "Are you pleased?"

She glanced back at the basket, bobbing on the water. "Reasonably. We had more trouble than I expected to align her to the target, even without a wind to trouble us. Now, we'll see how long she stays afloat." Her gaze came back to Julia. "Tea?"

"Of course! This way. I'm sure everyone will want to congratulate you."

Most of the assembled crowd began moving back toward the house, the servants at a more rapid pace to be ready for the guests. The two assistants remained by the lake, watching the balloon, notebooks and pencils in their hands. Lord Worthington could not seem to pull himself from their sides.

Tanner glanced around again. Everyone here was known to Mr. Hewett or Julia. He had spotted nothing amiss, but he strode to meet his colleagues, who had been watching at the opposite side and back of the crowd.

"Report," Roth barked, though he should have been following Tanner's lead for once. Tanner bristled, then forced himself to relax. It couldn't be easy relinquishing the reins of command. His father never had.

"Nothing unusual," Keller said with a look to Tanner. "Everyone seemed very pleased with the whole event." He grinned. "And it was something to tell our children about."

"Those of us who might have children," Roth reminded him. He looked pointedly at Tanner.

"You know my betrothal is a sham," he told him.

"It did not look like a sham from where I was standing," Roth said. "She chose to hold your hand."

Keller turned on him. "She did?"

"It was only the excitement of the moment," Tanner insisted. "Miss Hewett has no interest in me other than as a means to an end."

Roth did not look convinced. "So you saw nothing of concern either?"

"No," Tanner said. "And I'm just as glad. Why don't you both go in? I'd like a word with Lord Worthington."

Keller glanced toward the retreating group. "Are we to mix with the guests or the staff?"

"Both," Roth said before Tanner could answer. "I will take the staff. You take the guests."

Keller nodded. "That is to my liking. Miss Bee looked rather lovely today, did she not? The blue of her pelisse matched her eyes."

Tanner wasn't the only one staring at him.

Roth went so far as to cuff him on the shoulder. "Miss Bee is not your concern, unless she happens to be hiding a knife or gun under that pelisse. Now, go."

Ducking his head, Keller went. With a nod to Roth, Tanner turned for the lake.

Lord Worthington had managed to tear himself away from his work and was striding in his direction. Tanner fell in beside him to escort him to the house.

"It sounds as if all went well," Tanner ventured.

"Well indeed," he agreed. "Though I need a bit more tinkering with those foot pedals. They've been used in France to some effect, but I can't quite get the angle of them. Might be my legs." He chuckled.

"You were saying last night that you travel a great deal," Tanner ventured as they approached the house. "Do you ever require a bodyguard?"

"I had a bodyguard some years ago," he allowed, and Tanner's hopes rose. "I was receiving threatening notes at the time, and I worried for myself and my sister, who was working at my side. My bodyguard helped uncover the culprit, and my sister ended up marrying my bodyguard. Now she's Lady Bateman, after her husband saved the life of the Prince Regent and was made a baronet for his trouble. And I'm happy to say that there have been no threats on my life recently."

He glanced at Tanner as they reached the house. "But you cannot want to be my bodyguard and travel all over creation with us. You're about to be married."

"Yes, of course," Tanner said. He slowed his steps and allowed Lord Worthington to go ahead of him into the house.

He glanced around at the estate again. All seemed peaceful. Was the only danger here his growing feelings for Julia?

It took nearly two hours for their guests to finish congratulating Lord and Lady Worthington on their accomplishment. Julia had brought them all to the formal withdrawing room, which was the largest reception space in the house, and she'd instructed Garrison to keep the doors to the dining room open as well. Individuals and groups moved between the two rooms, sampling the drinks and cakes, biscuits, and cheeses on the long table and sharing their amazement with each other.

As hostess, Julia jumped from one group to the next, making sure everyone was comfortable and sociable. Daring had been cornered by Mrs. Godwin and couldn't seem to escape. Instead, Julia was surprised more than once to find Tanner at her side, directing her attention to this person and that group.

"Your Bees are buzzing," he murmured in her ear as she tried to keep her father from badgering Chester Godwin, their neighbor to the north, to invest in the railway.

She glanced about and sighted Miss Bee the elder standing alone by the hearth while her mother and sister monopolized the Worthingtons. Indeed, his lordship's face was beginning to resemble a thundercloud, and she could imagine those grey eyes flashing like lightning. Julia excused herself and hurried in that direction, Tanner at her side.

"And you really should allow guests to go up with you," Mrs. Bee was scolding the natural philosophers. "You're missing an opportunity to make a great deal of money."

"Ah, Mrs. Bee," Julia said, taking her arm, "just the expert I was hoping to find. I simply must hear your opinion on our new furnishings. You will pardon us."

Lady Worthington's smile was brilliant. "Why, of course."

"Thank you," Julia said to Tanner when she had finally managed to leave the lady spouting platitudes over their minister. Mr. Bradbury, at least, was used to fending her off, and he understood the need to keep her from imposing herself on the other guests. He was already nodding his balding head to some nonsense.

"Glad to be of service, if only in this small area," Tanner said.

"Hardly small," Julia assured him, tucking a stray hair back from her face. "You prevented bloodshed, sir! Does Batavaria have an award for heroism in the face of extreme danger?"

His smile was lighting his eyes again. "Certainly. Each of us has won it."

Julia grinned at him. "I can imagine that. But I think Mr. Keller might deserve a second commendation." She tipped her chin to where the young guardsman and Miss Bee were now chatting. The older sister's cheeks had pinked, and her shy smile was evident as Keller bent closer.

"Always one to throw himself into the fire," Tanner acknowledged, though his look was more thoughtful. "As are you. Perhaps we should find a commendation for hostesses."

Julia laughed.

She finally managed to send most of her guests home,

and Lord and Lady Worthington returned to the lake to see to their balloon. After requesting Julia's permission, Tanner had gone to join them. She and Daring climbed the stairs to her suite for a moment of quiet.

"A very successful event," Daring said as she went to one of the chairs by the hearth. "You should be pleased."

"I am," Julia told her. "But with you so valiantly dealing with Mrs. Godwin, I don't know what I would have done without Tanner."

Daring patted her navy skirts as Julia came to sit on the opposite chair. "I'm glad you still find him useful."

It was the second time she'd used that word for him. Daring made Tanner sound as if he were no more than a tortoiseshell comb or a silver-framed mirror.

"He's *more* than useful," Julia insisted. "I enjoy his company. He makes me laugh."

"There is something to be said for that," Daring allowed.

Julia frowned at her. "Do you dislike Mr. Tanner?"

Her companion smiled. "Certainly not, dear. He is intelligent and capable, and he knows when to sit and listen. I feel completely safe around him."

So did she. Not that she'd ever truly felt in danger. Oh, maybe once or twice when she'd misjudged a jump in riding or when her pony cart careened around a turn on one wheel. Tanner's presence made her feel as if she had a firm underpinning, a foundation from which to fly. She couldn't remember another suitor who had so raised her confidence.

"Is something wrong, dear?" Daring asked. "You've paled."

"Just tired," Julia said, unwilling to share the thought that had intruded. Tanner wasn't her suitor. Despite their claim to a betrothal, he wasn't going to marry her. Why had she put him in the same camp as Westie?

And why did the viscount come off looking decidedly less interesting in the process?

Saturday, they saw the Worthingtons, their staff, and all their belongings off.

"Where to now?" Julia asked Lady Worthington as her husband and Julia's father shook hands. Beside her, Tanner perked up.

"The Isle of Man," she confided. "Now that we've tried landing on a lake, Worth is keen to attempt it on saltwater."

"You couldn't find any closer?" Daring asked with a furrowed brow.

She laughed. "Where would be the fun in that?"

They all waved as the cavalcade started down the drive.

"And who is that coming?" Daring asked, peering under her bonnet brim toward the carriage approaching the house.

Tanner put a hand to Julia's elbow even as she stiffened. "That is the Bees' coach," he said.

She and Daring exchanged glances.

"We should check to make sure Lord and Lady Worthington forgot nothing at the lake," her companion said.

"Absolutely," Julia agreed, and the three of them turned for the side of the house.

"Oh, no you don't," her father said, stopping her in her tracks. "It's too late to escape now. They've likely spotted you. And you're not leaving me alone with that lot."

Julia slumped. "Oh, very well."

Tanner patted her shoulder in apparent sympathy. "I will remain at your side throughout."

"I must fetch my shawl," Daring said and darted into the house with surprising speed.

Julia pasted on a smile as the carriage came to a stop on the drive. One of her footmen went to open the door and lower the step. But instead of Mrs. Bee, the person who alighted was a small man with light-brown hair evident below his fashionable top hat. He turned to offer his hand to Elspeth.

"Louis," her father said, stepping forward. "I wasn't expecting you."

"Forgive the intrusion," he said in a gentle tenor voice. "I find myself in a difficult position, and I could use the advice of a friend."

"Certainly, certainly," her father said, taking his arm. "Come to my study. Our girls can chat."

"Actually," he said with a look to his daughter, "I'd like Elspeth to join us."

Elspeth turned to Julia, gaze pleading. "I don't believe you've met my father, Miss Hewett. Won't you and Mr. Tanner please join us as well?"

Put that way, she could hardly refuse, though her mind struggled with the idea that this quiet man was married to the demanding Mrs. Bee. She nodded, and the three of them followed her father and Mr. Bee into the house.

As if he thought they would be discussing business, her father led them to the study after they had all divested themselves of their coats and hats.

"Now, then," he said, waving them into seats as he went to his desk. "How can I help?"

There were only three other chairs in the room. Tanner moved to stand behind Julia's chair, allowing their unexpected guests to take the others.

"It is a matter of philosophy," Mr. Bee started. Now that his hat was off, she could see that his hair was thinning over a lined forehead, making him look perpetually worried. Equal lines fanned out from his eyes and mouth, and she could hope that meant he found time to laugh on occasion.

Her father barked a laugh now. "Philosophy? Then

you've mistaken your man. You passed our natural philosophers on the drive."

Mr. Bee's smile was as soft as his voice. "Not that sort of philosophy. My wife tells me the father is expected to arrange the marriage of any young lady with a fortune. She's been trying to help by providing me names of potential suitors." He glanced toward his daughter. "I find I simply don't have the stomach for it." His gaze came back to Julia's father. "How did you convince your girl to accept an Imperial Guard?"

Julia crossed her arms over her chest, waiting to see if her father would admit his hand in their engagement. Instead, he fiddled with a pencil on his desk.

"You and I are used to business dealings, Lou, my lad," he told their guest. "This is no different. You want a son-in-law you can be proud of."

"But not one you have to buy!" Julia protested, arms falling.

Her father pointed the pencil at her. "I don't recall our guest asking your opinion, young lady."

"Nor mine," Elspeth emboldened herself to say.

Mr. Bee grimaced. "You see the problem."

Her father tossed down the pencil. "I see it all right. Tanner, escort these ladies out. We fathers will discuss the best course forward."

It was a direct command from his employer, so Tanner would be forced to comply, but Julia vowed not to make it easy on him.

To her surprise, he shook his head. "I am always delighted to spend time in your daughter's company, Mr. Hewett. But when it comes to marriage, I strongly encourage you to listen to her opinions on the matter."

Her father flamed. "Out. The lot of you."

Tanner inclined his head.

Julia rose. "Come, Elspeth. You and I are much better company in any regard."

Elspeth rose and snapped a nod, and the two quit the room.

Tanner shut the door behind them. "Forgive me for speaking out of turn."

"No forgiveness necessary," Julia assured him. "I appreciate an ally."

"As do I," Elspeth said.

"I'll ask Mrs. Cheevers to send tea to the upstairs withdrawing room," he offered. With a bow, he left them.

"I thought your withdrawing room was on this floor," Elspeth said.

Julia thought for a moment about listening in on her father's conversation in the library and decided against it. Instead, she linked arms with her new friend. "The formal withdrawing room is where we entertain callers. Friends and family visit us in the upstairs withdrawing room."

"You are too kind," Elspeth said with a sweet smile that quickly faded as they started up the stairs. "I'm so sorry my father came to see yours. It was all my fault."

"Because you chose to have an opinion as to whom you wed?" Julia challenged. She escorted her friend to the sofa and sat beside her.

"Because I told him I was beginning to have feelings for a certain gentleman," Elspeth confessed, dropping her gaze to her hands folded in the lap of her sky-blue wool gown.

Julia grinned. "Oh, wonderful! Who?"

Elspeth's smile was knowing. "I am not at liberty to say. Just know that you have inspired me. Perhaps you will have the opportunity to dance with him at the assembly tonight."

"Tonight!" Julia clapped her hand to her mouth.

"You didn't forget," Elspeth said, sounding a bit like her mother. "It's the last assembly until the new year."

Julia lowered her hand. "Yes, of course. It's just with the

balloon ascension and the railway opening, I haven't had time to choose a gown. Nothing's been pressed. There are probably hems that need stitching."

Elspeth took her hand. "Then let us put aside my troubles and see to your wardrobe. No lady wants to appear dowdy in front of her betrothed."

Would Tanner care what she wore? Would he even notice? Why did she suddenly care very much indeed?

Julia rose. "Come with me. I would relish your advice."

CHAPTER ELEVEN

TANNER RETURNED WITH Quinn, the footman, who was armed with a silver tea tray, only to find the withdrawing room empty.

"Downstairs?" Quinn asked with a frown.

"You check the formal withdrawing room, I'll check the library and study," Tanner said with a shake of his head.

Julia's whims would be the death of him. She offered friendship quickly and didn't hesitate to open her heart. Her mind worked as quickly. Why didn't she understand that he needed to know where she was and with whom to protect her?

He found no one in the library, so eased open the study door just enough to be certain the two fathers were alone, then closed it and glanced to the footman across the entry hall. "Any luck, Quinn?"

"Empty, sir," he said with a shrug that set the teacups to chiming.

"See if Mr. Hewett wants the tea," Tanner said.

Quinn nodded.

Doubts gnawed at Tanner as he climbed the stairs two at a time. No one would accost her here. Surely if one of the staff had sent that threatening note, the person would have acted on it by now. But what if Julia had left the house, gone for a carriage ride with Miss Bee? They'd be easy prey for the highwaymen. They might not carry gold with them, but their jewelry alone would be worth the effort.

Pepin was sitting in a corner of Tanner's room, tongue stuck out of one corner of his mouth, as he attempted to sew a button back on a waistcoat.

"I need you to go to the stables," Tanner told him. "See if Miss Hewett has gone out."

The lad jumped up so fast he winced as the needle must have nicked. "I would, sir, but Miss Hewett, Miss Bee, and Mrs. Daring are in her room. I came up with Candy, Miss Hewett's maid, when she was sent for."

Tension fled like rain before a thundercloud. "Good lad. Thank you."

Clearly mystified, Pepin reached for the waistcoat.

Tanner found the ladies in Julia's suite. Once again, clothing littered the furniture, only this time it consisted of gowns of various colors, materials, and styles.

"This Saxon green silk is lovely," Miss Bee was saying, fingering a frothy confection the color of sage, which was draped over a chair by the hearth.

"It's one of my favorites," Julia confessed. "But it's more suited to a summer ball. In fact, the last time I wore it…" Her face turned pink.

He remembered. In a moonlit garden, with the sounds of the ball coming softly from the castle, it had been easy to think he'd found a faery of legend. She'd been perched on a stone bench, head bowed and shoulders shaking, and nothing could have stopped him from offering aid. He should have been on patrol, watching for trouble. Little had he dreamed trouble would appear in the form of a sylph in a sage-colored gown.

"So many to choose from," Mrs. Daring put in. "What do you think, Mr. Tanner?"

Julia whirled to find him standing in the doorway. He didn't look nearly as discomposed as she felt at the reminder of their first meeting. His face was as smooth and still as usual.

"Yes, Mr. Tanner," Elspeth said, dropping her hand and straightening with a smile. "You must have an opinion on what your beloved should wear."

He strolled closer, and Julia took a step to meet him, then froze. What was wrong with her? She wasn't his beloved, and she certainly didn't need a gentleman telling her which gown to choose!

"Julia always looks beautiful to me," he said. "I would no more tell her how to dress than tell a rose how to bloom."

He was playing a part and doing it very well. There was no need for her to gaze at him in wonder. But that knowledge didn't seem to stop her.

"Well said, sir!" Elspeth enthused.

Julia shook herself. "The cinnamon-colored satin, I think. It's more suited to autumn." She turned to her waiting maid. "Can you have it ready in time, Candy?"

The dark-haired maid lifted the gown into her arms. "I'll go press it this minute, Miss Hewett." She curtseyed and left.

Elspeth looked to Julia. "I should see if Father's ready to go. I can only hope this visit hasn't sealed my fate."

"Stay strong," Julia told her. "I'll see you tonight."

"Let me take you down, dear," Daring said, and she showed their guest out, leaving Julia and Tanner alone.

"I will miss seeing the sage again," he said.

Julia stared at him. "You remember?"

"I remember every moment in your company," he said. When she gaped again, one side of his mouth lifted. "It is expected of a bodyguard."

Oh, but he could be maddening!

Of course, so could her father. He came to see her after

Elspeth and Mr. Bee had left and Daring had returned to help Julia put the other dresses back into their clothes presses.

"That's done, then," he said. "I hear you're attending the assembly. Perhaps the Marquess of Norfall will be there."

Julia glared at him. "I thought we'd agreed that I would make my own choices. But then again, you spent the afternoon advising Mr. Bee how to rule over his daughter. Father, how could you!"

He puffed out his chest. "You have no concept of what we fathers go through to see our daughters well settled. Small wonder we need to commiserate once in a while."

As she sputtered, he turned to Tanner, who was standing at guard near the door. "I've matters to attend to. You'll make sure she gets there and back safely."

He clapped his fist to his chest and inclined his head.

But at least he sat inside the coach that night when she and Daring set out.

"Let me guess," Julia said, hands bunched in the folds of her black velvet evening cloak. "Father also charged you to make sure I didn't escape."

"Oh, were we planning to run away?" Daring asked, closing her own cloak over her puce satin skirts. "I fear I'm not dressed for it."

"It's too cold and dark to run away," Tanner assured them from his side of the coach. "Too dark to see a highwayman coming as well, which is why I elected to ride inside. Besides, I plan to play a devoted fiancé tonight."

Julia sighed. "I warn you, Tanner, I'm in no mood to be ordered about."

He cocked his head. "Is that how your other suitors treated you?"

"Some tried," Daring muttered. "Poor fools."

"I had some very presentable suitors," Julia protested.

"They complimented my looks; they escorted me wherever I wanted to go. One even composed an ode in my honor."

Tanner snorted.

"What? Think you can do better?" she challenged.

Daring's hands began fluttering.

"If I were courting," Tanner said, gaze darkening, "my lady would have no doubt of my regard. Any man can appreciate outer beauty. I would know her well enough to compliment her on her character and accomplishments. We would share activities we both enjoyed, our enjoyment multiplied simply by being together. And I would have no call to compose poetry when I felt free to offer words from my heart."

Goodness! "I envy the lady who attracts your attention," Julia said.

His gaze went out the window. "I believe we have arrived."

And a very good thing too, or she might have thrown herself across the coach and into his arms.

What had possessed him to prattle on about courtship? Yes, it was a topic often debated among men forced to watch from the wall. Yes, he had once instructed Lord Ashforde on the topic when his lordship had been courting Petunia Bateman, Lady Moselle, and doing it badly for all the lady favored him. Tanner had no right to state an opinion on courtship to Julia when he had no right to court her or any woman at the moment.

So, he focused on his duty. He had attended the assembly in October with Lady Belfort; her companion at the time, Abigail Winchester; and the other guards, so he was familiar with the arrangement. A wide corridor with coat and retiring rooms on either side led to the octagon-shaped ballroom with its butter-colored walls, white molding cast in leafy swirls, and musicians' alcove over the entry door. One of the doors off the ballroom gave onto a long, narrow supper room, and another opened to a card room. Voices rose and fell like waves, and the air was a mixture of ladies' perfume, gentlemen's cologne, and candle wax.

Given the number of attendees and their constant movement, the line of sight was challenging at best. And given Julia's tendency to dart off on a tangent, he foresaw a long night.

Then he spotted Keller moving toward him, escorting Lady Belfort. Like Tanner, his friend had worn the black evening coat and knee breeches expected of a gentleman. Lady Belfort was in her usual lavender, this frock with a profusion of lace down the front.

"Meredith!" Julia hailed, taking her hand. "I thought we'd never find you. Excellent attendance. Unfortunately, as I feared, we have more ladies than gentlemen."

"Mr. Tanner and Mr. Keller will be much sought after," Lady Belfort predicted.

Tanner put a hand to Julia's elbow. "No need for concern. Either Keller or I will attend you."

"If you can keep up," she teased with a grin. "I intend to dance every dance."

Tanner bent closer and caught the scent of lilacs. "Then I will break your English rule about no more than two dances for a partner."

She regarded him from under her lashes. "Why, Tanner, how bold."

Those lips were only inches away. If he just dipped his head a little more…

"I do believe the first dance is about to start, dear," Mrs. Daring said.

Tanner jerked upright. What, had he been about to kiss Julia in public? Even betrothed couples were seldom so obvious in their affections here in England. And everyone around him knew that they were not really betrothed.

Julia didn't seem affected. She seized his hand and pulled him out onto the floor.

Her quicksilver nature meant that on the dancefloor she had no equal. It was as if the sun had returned to Surrey in all its summer glory. She swished her skirts in time with the tune, smiling at him from across the line as if encouraging him closer. When it was their turn, she skipped down the line like a lamb crossing a spring meadow. As he spun her on his arm, her giggle rewarded him. Every lady smiled; every gentleman looked at her in admiration. And more than one glanced at Tanner with envy stamped on his face.

"Mr. Keller's turn," she announced after two line dances with Tanner. They had returned to Lady Belfort only a moment. The lady herself had danced with Mr. Godwin, and Mrs. Daring was out on the arm of a retired colonel.

Julia glanced around. "Where *is* Mr. Keller?"

Lady Belfort nodded to the other side of the room. "I have heard of bees to honey, but never of honey to a Bee."

Tanner frowned as his friend bowed over the hand of Miss Bee the elder. By the looks crossing her mother's and sister's face, neither lady knew whether to be pleased or dismayed by his attentions. He led Julia's friend out onto the dancefloor.

"I'm not sure Fortune would approve," Lady Belfort murmured, watching as Miss Bee simpered at Keller.

"Elspeth is perfectly delightful when you get her away from her mother," Julia assured her. "She told me she had a suitor she favored, one her parents did not approve either. It appears Mr. Keller is her choice."

Tanner tipped up his chin in warning, then smiled politely. "Good evening, Lord Norfall."

Julia's cheeks turned pink, clashing with her gown, but

she held her head high as the marquess joined them. He had chosen a navy coat and cream-colored breeches, but the watch chain crossing his wine-colored waistcoat had so many fobs on it that Tanner could only wonder if the fellow jingled when he danced.

"Good evening, Miss Hewett, Lady Belfort, Mr. Tanner," the marquess greeted in his nasally voice. "Did I hear someone say that Miss Bee has chosen a suitor?"

"I'm certain I cannot speak for Miss Bee, my lord," Julia said.

"Ah, of course," he said. "One must support one's friends. Forgive the interruption. I don't generally attend such events, but Lord Westerbrook advised me it is the done thing when courting." He glanced about. "I expected him as well."

Tanner nearly sagged. The presence of the viscount was all the night needed.

"I do not believe he is in Surrey at present," Julia told him. "But please give him my regards when next you see him."

"Delighted." He bowed to Julia. "Would you care to dance, Miss Hewett?"

Once again, she seized Tanner's arm. "I fear I cannot, my lord. I promised dear Tanner a promenade."

The fellow still must not have been told about Tanner and Julia's faux engagement, for he frowned. Lady Belfort, bless her, shifted on her feet, setting her skirts to swaying.

The marquess quickly turned to her. "And you, my dear?"

"You honor me," Lady Belfort said. She accepted his arm and sailed out onto the dancefloor, but the look she shot back at Tanner let him know that he would owe her a favor.

"We should promenade," Julia said beside him. "I don't wish to appear a liar."

The words echoed inside him. Her father had agreed

that Tanner could tell Julia about their agreement at the right time. Might now be that time?

"Funny thing about lying," he started, taking her arm and moving along the edge of the room. "Sometimes it isn't so much a lie but a withholding of information."

She frowned at him. "They seem the same to me."

Tanner swallowed. But before he could continue, he spotted more trouble heading their way. "Do you play cards?" he asked.

Julia's frown only grew. "Certainly."

"Good," he said, turning them for the card room at a clip that made at least one doyen raise her quizzing glass in surprise. "Because that may be the only way to avoid the attentions of the Bees."

Tanner managed to finish the evening and return Julia and Mrs. Daring to the house with all fingers and toes intact. They had avoided a confrontation with Mrs. Bee, and Julia had not been forced to partner the marquess in either cards or the dance. She called the night a success.

He wasn't so sure. The more time he spent with her, the more he found to admire. But, between her devotion to Lord Westerbrook and her father's fixation on a title, Tanner had little hope of making their false engagement real.

The matter remained on his mind as they all headed for church on Sunday. He turned up his collar and pulled down on his hat against a misty rain as he hunkered on the bench with Towser. At least there was no sign of trouble, until they drew up on the lane in front of the church. Parishioners stood in clusters, faces pale, but hands moving.

"Something's happened," Tanner told the coachman. "Go ahead and stop, but wait for my signal before leaving."

"Right you are, sir," Towser said.

As the horses pulled up, Tanner hopped down. Lady Belfort and his fellow guards must have already arrived, for Keller strode to meet him.

"Another robbery," he told Tanner, mist collecting on his tall-crowned hat. "Just last night, from what I hear. Highwaymen, as before." He glanced around the churchyard as if expecting the thieves to come striding out from behind a gravestone.

"Help me get Miss Hewett and the others into the church," Tanner said.

Keller nodded.

"What is it?" Julia asked as soon as her feet hit the muddy ground. "You look worried."

He must be out of practice that she could spot his concern. He made himself offer a polite smile as her father climbed down as well.

"There's been a robbery," he explained. "We should be safe in church, but stay close, just in case."

Mr. Hewett nodded, Mrs. Daring stepped closer, and Julia latched onto Tanner's arm.

Warmth radiated from her touch, but it wasn't from her proximity. He'd escorted any number of ladies, in far more dangerous circumstances, and never felt such pleasure to be trusted. He tore his gaze from her face as Keller came alongside her father. He signaled to Towser, then he and Keller walked his charges into the church.

Even there, voices murmured in what was usually a silence broken only by the rustle of cloth or the creak of a pew. More than one gaze was aimed at the Duke of Wey near the front. As the highest-ranking peer in the area, he would not normally act as magistrate, Lady Belfort had told the guards, but he was serving in that function until a new one was appointed. Either position would make him keen to see no trouble in his district.

Mr. Bradbury, the vicar, appeared just as concerned, for he preached a rousing sermon about the dangers of coveting thy neighbors' goods. What, did he think the highwaymen members of his own congregation? Tanner couldn't help glancing around, but no one was shifting with guilt or turning pale to be singled out. More likely, they were nodding in agreement.

"Who was it, do you know?" Julia asked Lady Belfort when they met her and Keller after the service. Roth was already making a tour of the periphery, ensuring the safety of their patroness.

Before her ladyship could answer Julia, Mrs. Bee hurried over, her daughters trailing. Her eyes were bright under her feathered hat, and one hand was pressed against the lace peeking out of the neck of her satin pelisse.

"Oh, the horror of it," she proclaimed. "Robbed, in sight of his own home! You must be more generous with your Imperial Guards, Lady Belfort, or we shall all be murdered!"

"I am quite sure Mr. Tanner, Mr. Keller, and Mr. Roth are available to any who might need them," Lady Belfort said with a quelling look in her direction. "When they are not engaged with their own professions."

"In sight of his own home, you say?" Mr. Hewett put in. "Who was it?"

Mrs. Bee's face lit at a chance to be the most important person in the conversation. "None other than the Marquess of Norfall. He was attacked on his way home from the assembly!"

CHAPTER TWELVE

THE MARQUESS OF Norfall? Tanner shook his head. Why would thieves attack a peer?

Julia's father apparently had similar concerns, for he paled. "I'll speak with the duke." He stalked off.

"Much good it will do him," Mrs. Bee predicted. "I've spoken with His Grace any number of times about the matter, but he does not seem disposed to listen. But then, I suppose he is safe in that great castle of his on the island. What of the rest of us!"

"Perhaps Mr. Keller could come live with us as Mr. Tanner does with Miss Hewett, Mama," Miss Bee the younger said, swishing her skirts so that they brushed Keller's boots.

Tanner had a sudden urge to tug his friend out of harm's way.

Miss Bee the elder must have had a similar thought, for she stepped between her sister and Keller. "Nonsense, Angelica. We must all be brave against these bullies."

"Well said, Miss Bee," Keller told her, gaze so admiring Tanner almost elbowed him.

She pinked, lashes fluttering like Mrs. Daring's hands.

Roth must have finished his patrol, for he rejoined them. "I have spoken with His Grace. Keller and I will be helping him hunt down these villains."

Mrs. Bee nodded. "Serves them right."

Her younger daughter clasped her hands in front of her rose-colored redingote. "Oh, Mr. Keller, how brave!"

Her sister gazed at Keller with her pale blue eyes. "You will be careful?"

"Of course," Keller said with a smile. "I would not want to jeopardize my future, not now that I have reason to hope."

Mrs. Bee frowned at him. Oh, but his friend was standing on the edge of a sword. Had his sweetheart not told him of her parents' plan for her? Or did he simply not care?

Mr. Hewett returned to them just then.

"His Grace and the other Imperial Guards have the matter in hand," he said. "No need for concern." He glanced toward the south. "Shame about Norfall, though. I'll have Garrison send some of those late apples over."

Tanner still couldn't accept the story. Wherever he had lived, the laws for robbing such personages were strict— deportation at a minimum and sometimes beheading or hanging. He couldn't imagine they were any lesser in England. Why take such a chance? Or had they not known who they were troubling? What of Keller's assertion that they were studying their victims?

"And what news of your dear husband, Lady Belfort?" Julia's father was asking.

The lady's lavender eyes turned down. "They are still waiting for Württemberg to ratify the agreement."

Keller glanced between her and Roth. "They would not go back on their word."

"They might," Roth muttered.

"I'm certain it's merely a momentary delay," Lady Belfort said, chin coming up. "Julian wouldn't allow otherwise."

"Neither would the king," Keller said with a grin to Tanner.

King Frederick was big and brash and bold, and even exile had not been able to beat that out of him. Now that his kingdom was being returned to him, he would likely be the one pushing for the agreement to be made final.

"With any luck, Lord Belfort will be home before Christmas," Julia encouraged their patroness.

"Will you be hosting your lovely Christmas Eve party again, Lady Belfort?" Miss Bee asked eagerly.

Lady Belfort's smile was cool. "I have yet to decide. Rest assured, invitations will go out to the appropriate guests as soon as I know my own mind."

"See that you're on that list, my girl," Julia's father told her after they'd made their excuses and were walking toward the coach. "You have every right to attend Lady Belfort's party."

"She has never left me off before, Father," Julia reminded him. "I've been attending since Mother was alive."

His face slumped a moment, but he quickly recovered. "Right, then. Let's head for home. Tanner, keep an eye out for any trouble."

"Of course," he said, putting his hand to the coach.

"Couldn't he ride inside with us, Father?" Julia asked, gaze turned up to his employer. "The weather is turning beastly."

As if to prove as much, the wind shook the nearby trees, and Towser settled himself deeper on the seat.

"With these highwaymen about, I wouldn't chance it," her father said. "He's a strong lad. He'll be fine."

Julia offered Tanner a regretful look before climbing into the coach with Mrs. Daring and her father.

Tanner remained watchful as they drove out of Weyton and onto the Weybridge Road. Most of the way it was fields on all sides, divided by hedgerows. The only trees were at either edge of the Hewett estate. The one copse closer to the village would have made an excellent hiding place for the highwaymen, but he saw no sign of miscreants there either.

Quinn was kind enough to take his sodden coat when they arrived back at Hewett House, though Garrison continued to pretend Tanner didn't exist. He made sure to shrug out of the coat in such a way that a few drops fell onto the butler's spotless leather shoes. Garrison's jaw tightened.

"Will you be in the library?" Tanner asked Julia as she settled her skirts.

"Reading a book, yes," she answered, glancing up. "Why?"

"I need a moment with your father."

Her eyes widened as he stepped away.

Mr. Hewett had already adjourned to his favorite room and was at his desk, papers spread before him. Tanner waited in the doorway to be acknowledged. It took a few moments.

Finally, her father glanced up, and the hollowness in his eyes forced Tanner into the room.

"How did you know?" Hewett croaked.

Tanner faced him across the desk. "Know what?"

"That I'd received another threatening note."

"I didn't," Tanner said. "I came to ask if you'd allow me to join the duke in hunting down the highwaymen." He nodded to the piece of paper gripped in his employer's hand. "May I?"

Hewett thrust it at him as if he couldn't bear to hold on.

I have had enough of your interference. You think these highwaymen are a nuisance? Wait until they come for your daughter.

If he had fallen through ice on the skating pond, Tanner could not have been colder. "When did this arrive?"

"I found it just now," Hewett said. "It was among the letters that came by yesterday's post, like the last."

"Then we need to speak to whoever picked up the post," Tanner said.

Hewett rose and strode to the door. "Garrison!"

Tanner turned the note in his hand. No one had mentioned that the others who had been robbed had received threatening notes first, but if none of the victims had shared the fact, who would know? Yet why would highwaymen warn their victims in advance? Wouldn't that just ensure they were more heavily protected?

The butler returned with his employer.

"Who's been bringing the post?" Hewett demanded, remaining on his feet.

"Whoever is available, sir," Garrison said, back ramrod straight and gaze on the far paneling. "Is there a problem?"

"Someone has been inserting threatening notes with the letters," Tanner explained. "We need to determine who."

"No one in this house would threaten Mr. Hewett," Garrison said, lip curling.

"It's not me they're threatening," Hewett said. "It's Julia."

Garrison washed white as his gaze jerked back to his employer's. "I can assure you, sir, that everyone in the household holds Miss Hewett in the highest regard."

"And you can vouch for them personally?" Tanner pressed.

Garrison's cheek ticked as he looked to Tanner at last. "Yes, every last one. Except you."

Hewett sucked in a breath. "That's enough on that score. The first note arrived before Mr. Tanner ever set foot in this house. It's one of the reasons I hired him."

"Convenient when your employer finds such an urgent need for your services," Garrison drawled.

"It won't wash," Hewett insisted. "No one knew I was thinking about approaching Lady Belfort or which guard she might offer me. More than one was available, if memory serves."

"Keller had yet to find a position, and Roth was wondering about his," Tanner supplied.

"As you say, sir," Garrison said.

"Who picked up the mail yesterday?" Tanner asked, determined to run the culprit down despite the butler's protests.

"Pulvey," Garrison said. "I'll ask him to speak to you, sir."

Hewett nodded, and Garrison turned on his heel and left without another look to Tanner.

"Have you been having trouble with that one?" Julia's father asked as he returned to his desk.

"Nothing I cannot handle," Tanner said.

Hewett grinned, sitting on his chair and leaning back. "I'd like to see that boxing match. I know who I'd put my money on." Then he shook his head. "But I'd like to see this matter settled far more. You asked to help the duke track down these highwaymen, and I'm sorely tempted to let you do it. But Julia needs you. She must be our focus now, my lad. Let nothing deter you."

"Pulvey has gone in now," Daring reported from the library doorway. She carefully shut the door while Julie set her ear once more to the pale paneling.

Someone was inserting threatening notes in the post, Tanner had said. And then her father had claimed they threatened her! Even Garrison had sounded shocked by the fact. She had never heard his voice shake like that. Of course, it could have been the effect of trying to overhear through the woodwork.

The poor footman was no better. His voice was so weak she only understood that he had no idea a note had been among the letters. Tanner promised to speak to the postmaster in the village on Monday.

"They're dispersing," she told Daring, scrambling away from the wall. "Hurry! We need to put away the books."

She and Daring began shoving the titles back onto the shelf while Julia quickly relayed the gist of the conversation she'd overheard.

"At least you know Mr. Tanner wasn't asking to marry you," Daring said.

"Worse luck," Julia muttered, pushing on a spine.

Daring's brows went up.

"I don't know where that came from," Julia assured her, shutting the glass door. "Besides, he wouldn't ask Father to marry me. Father already thinks we're engaged."

"Hmm," Daring mused.

But Julia had missed part of the conversation, she was sure of it. Somehow, she didn't think she could coerce her father into confessing.

But maybe she could convince Tanner to tell all.

When he came in a few moments later, she was seated by the hearth, book held right-side up this time, with Daring standing beside the opposite bookcase, studying the books there as if trying to determine which to read next.

"Ah," Julia said, setting the book aside and rising. "There you are. The weather's blown itself out. I'm for a ride. Would you join me?"

"Of course," he said smoothly.

Daring covered her mouth with one hand. "You'll have to forgive me. A nap is calling."

"You go right ahead," Julia said with a fond smile. She really was the best companion. "I'm sure I'll be perfectly safe with Tanner."

That he was not nearly so sure was evident by the fact that he asked two of the grooms to come along when Julia had changed into her riding habit and walked with him to the stables. They seemed mystified, but of course they were willing. She would hardly get him to tell her the truth with witnesses!

She put a hand on his arm. "It's nothing but fields," she reminded him. "We can see any trouble coming from nearly a mile away. Surely we needn't trouble these gentlemen."

The two grooms nodded hopefully.

Tanner's jaw worked, but he finally agreed. A short time later, the two of them were cantering across the fields. Though the wind still moved the trees that marked the edge of the property, the sun was pushing through the clouds, leaving them rimmed with silver.

"You seem unaccountably tense, Mr. Tanner," she told him as they slowed to a walk. "Truly, we should be in no danger here. One of the reasons Father chose this property was the extensive view. He said he'd worked in coal pits too long to ever want to feel confined again."

"It is a fine view," he allowed, gaze swinging from the Weybridge Road on the left to the lake on their right.

"Then why are you so concerned?" Julia pressed.

"I am your bodyguard. I'm merely doing my duty."

She patted her horse's dark neck. "Edevane would never allow anything to hurt me."

"I'm not concerned about rabbit holes in the field," he said. "There are other dangers afoot."

"Tell me."

He glanced her way, and for a moment she thought he would lie to her. The idea made her feel like squirming on the saddle. Whatever else they might claim to be, she and Tanner were becoming friends. Surely they could count on each other.

"Your father has been receiving unsigned threatening notes," he said. "They come with the post, but there is no sign they came *through* the post."

Interesting. "So, no postmarks or franking?" Julia asked.

His smile curved up as if he were impressed with her knowledge. "Neither. It is fine paper, and whoever is sending it knows enough to cut it so as to eliminate or obscure any watermark."

"Someone with income, then," she surmised. "Any misspellings?"

"Not a one." He sounded distinctly disappointed by the fact. "Your father and I have concluded that the writer has education as well. And he doesn't recognize the handwriting."

"Perhaps I should see them," she said, guiding Edevane around a thicker hillock of grass. "I might recognize the handwriting."

He regarded her. "An excellent suggestion. I'll have you review them as soon as we return."

"Are they particularly vile?" she asked. "Not that I don't want to read them. I'd just like to be prepared."

"They are surprisingly vague," Tanner said, lip curling in obvious distaste. "Although the most recent one connected them to the highwaymen."

"What!" Julia shook her head. "That cannot be right. Highwaymen don't go around penning perfectly written warning letters."

He shrugged. "I thought the same, but they needn't be without education. People of all classes can fall on hard times."

"So hard they can purchase fancy paper? Doubtful."

He glanced her way. "Your father thinks it may be one of his competitors."

Julia stiffened, and Edevane tossed his head. She settled onto the saddle.

"It must be that man I saw," she said, "the one I told you about."

"That man was Rufus Jacobs," he explained. "A canal builder from Weybridge. He was one of the highwaymen's victims. He was lying in bed, unconscious, the last time I heard."

A shiver went through her. "Then some other competitor? You should ask Father about them. I'm sure he has dozens."

"So it seems. I wouldn't be surprised if the fellow didn't show up at the railway opening. I've asked Keller and Roth to go with us to protect you."

Julia reined in, and he drew his horse to a stop beside Edevane.

"No! Not to protect me!" she cried. "We should try to trap him! I can be the bait."

Once more he shook his head. "Don't ask me to put you in danger."

Julia frowned. "Why not? I know you're supposed to be my bodyguard, and I'm sure it's a point of pride to keep me safe. But the best way to keep me safe, it would seem to me, is to capture whoever is threatening me. Besides, it's not as if we're really engaged."

"No," he said, eyes suddenly stormier than the sky. "Very likely, we will never be engaged. I am only your bodyguard. But I'm coming to care for you more than a bodyguard should." He leaned across the space and kissed her.

She could have pulled back. She could have urged Edevane away. Tanner would never have caught them. But the touch of his lips raised a yearning inside her, a wish to hold this moment close, to hold him close.

Could she be falling in love with Tanner? That would never do. If Father would not countenance a viscount, he would never agree to let her wed her bodyguard.

He'd broken the most important rule of being a bodyguard: Never become attached to those you guard. He should be ashamed to have given in to his feelings and kissed Julia. He should be furious with himself for allowing emotion to overcome good sense.

But all he wanted to do was kiss her again.

He pulled back and watched as she opened her eyes and stared at him. What was that emotion swirling in that warm brown gaze?

Her horse shimmied away, and she took a moment to get the stallion back under control. By the time she came alongside Tanner again, it was obvious she had herself under control as well.

"We will not speak of this," she said. "It was a momentary aberration on both our parts. You know the path toward your future, and I know the path toward mine, and this, this, whatever it is, helps neither of us."

She was absolutely right and far more generous than some ladies would have been. But he could not help the disappointment that settled over him. "Of course," he said, inclining his head.

She turned her horse for the house. "We should get back. We have much to do if we're to have a trap ready to spring at the railway opening."

If she could remain focused on her goal, so could he. He turned his horse to join her. "I did not agree to that."

"Remind me again, what is the role of a bodyguard?" she asked sweetly, head cocked so that her riding hat slipped on her red hair. "I would think the employer's wishes would override other considerations."

He smiled. "Your father is my employer. Perhaps we should ask him."

She huffed. "He'll never agree. Oh, but the pair of you are maddening!"

Normally, he would have protested being categorized with a man who insisted even on the fellow she should wed, but at the moment he didn't mind. So long as it kept her safe.

CHAPTER THIRTEEN

TANNER MADE SURE to escort Julia to her father's study as soon as they returned to the house, where he requested that she be shown the notes.

Hewett rolled his eyes. "You had to tell her."

"I prefer not to lie to your daughter, sir," Tanner reminded him.

His huff was merely a deeper version of hers. "Very well, though I'm not sure why you'd want to see them, Julia." He went to take both from the box on the mantel and offered them to his daughter.

She looked at first one, then the other. She shook her head as she handed them back to her father. "I don't recall seeing this handwriting before. Sorry."

"Just as well," her father said, tucking them away. "At least we know it isn't an acquaintance."

"It isn't anyone who's written to me more than a few times," she corrected him. "That's a relatively small number of my acquaintances. Still, I would hope none of them would go so far as to engage highwaymen to accost me!"

"Oh, I don't know," her father said, turning to face her with a grin. "Have you annoyed Daring sufficiently lately?"

"Father!" she protested, then she gave a laugh. "Very likely I've annoyed poor Daring to distraction any number of times. But I've seen her handwriting, and that doesn't match. I've been trying to convince Tanner that we should use the railway opening as an opportunity to trap the miscreant."

Her father's smile faded into a frown. "And how do you propose we do that?"

"She wants to put herself in a position to be accosted," Tanner said.

Her father drew himself up. "Here, now! There'll be none of that, my girl. I didn't hire you a bodyguard so you could go around putting yourself in danger."

She glanced at Tanner, brows coming down. "And perhaps I wouldn't need a bodyguard if we resolved the danger."

"No," her father said, just as she'd predicted and Tanner had hoped. "You leave this matter to Tanner and me."

She tossed her head and swept from the room.

"Keep an eye on her," Hewett said. "She may well come up with a plan all on her own."

"Then I must do my best to solve this mystery before she does," Tanner said. With a nod to his employer, he strode after Julia.

When he had been guarding King Frederick and his sons, one of his duties had been to stand along the wall at court functions, keeping an eye out for trouble. It had been a pleasure to be allowed to sit when he had been guarding Lady Belfort and her companion, Abigail, but after that kiss, a little distance from Julia might be wise. Accordingly, he located her and Mrs. Daring in the upstairs withdrawing room and took up a position in one corner, where he could see the door, the windows, and his charge.

Julia regarded him. "Mr. Huber used to do that when Abigail and Lady Belfort visited. I never found it comforting."

"A shame," he said, keeping his gaze moving.

"It is a standard practice, dear," Mrs. Daring told her.

"I'm only surprised Mr. Tanner has agreed to sit with us as often as he has."

His mistake. He would not make it again.

Julia appeared to be doing her best to ignore him the rest of the day and Monday morning, going about her business with head high and steps purposeful. She and Mrs. Daring intended to spend time answering correspondence about the various charities she supported, meaning they would be safely at the house. That gave him a moment to journey in to Weyton and speak with the postmaster.

Mr. Summers had the snow-colored hair of experience and the arms of a seasoned pugilist. He shook his head when Tanner asked him about the post.

"All mail comes right here," he said, pointing to a sack behind him. "Brought by the mail coach every day. His Grace, the Duke of Wey, insists on it. I sort it, or I have my assistant do so, into these boxes." He indicated a honeycomb of shelving to one side. "And I only give it to a known representative of the household for which it is intended."

"And you've seen nothing without a postmark or franking?" Tanner pressed.

He pursed his lips. "We do get one slip through on occasion. So long as the address is clear, I send it on."

"Any for Hewett House?"

"Two in the last month. Most odd."

So, the letters could have been placed in the post in London or at any of the stops in between, so long as the postmaster there hadn't noticed. He'd put his money on London, with its busier offices. That still left a number of Hewett's competitors and Julia's. Surely more than one young lady on the marriage mart, as the English called it, resented her beauty and fortune.

But he was no closer to the answer as to whom.

Tanner continued to hover. He was always along the wall during Julia's activities at home and at her side should she decide to ride. He remained in the formal withdrawing room as she held her at-home on Tuesday, earning him more than one curious look from her callers.

"I understood he was your betrothed, Miss Hewett," Mrs. Godwin said with a frown. "I would have loved to have trained my Chester to stand about quietly like that. However did you manage it?"

"It is a Batavarian custom," Daring said for her. "I doubt you could find an Englishman so compliant."

Julia was certain she heard Tanner grinding his teeth.

He was even worse on Wednesday at the railway opening. The rails ran from the warehouses at Walton-on-Thames to others in Lambeth, on the south bank of the Thames from London. Today, the trip would only be as far as Molesley, a few miles away, with a view across the river to Hampton Court. More than three dozen people were gathered beside the engine and its string of open cars, one of which had been fitted with seats for the short ride. She spotted Lord and Lady Worthington, the latter chatting happily with one of the engineers; Mr. and Mrs. Bee and their daughters, all of whom looked impressed; and Mr. Roth and Mr. Keller, who were glancing about with watchful eyes. Tanner kept one hand on her elbow as she, Daring, and her father moved from the carriage to the wide, rough planks of the platform.

The Stephenson engine was a squat beast, with a fat black boiler and a short stack already belching out clouds of steam. It clutched at the rails that stretched out into the distance like a raven come to roost. Some workers with handkerchiefs up over their mouths and noses shoveled coal into the greedy maw of the engine. She could understand the need for protection. The air was tainted with the whiff of brimstone.

As Julia's father excused himself to speak with the engineers, Meredith made her way to their sides, one hand lifting her lavender skirts.

"Another veritable crush," she declared with a smile. She glanced around, setting the ostrich plume in her hat to swaying, then leaned closer. "Were you able to convince Lord Westerbrook to come meet Fortune?"

At least she'd remembered to write to him. "I haven't heard," Julia confessed. "I hope he'll tell me today."

"That cat always knows the worth of a person," Tanner mused. "I will be interested in seeing what she thinks of your viscount."

Her viscount. Clearly, Tanner's heart was not engaged if he could call Lord Westerbrook that. No, she must not think of him as Lord Westerbrook. He had asked her to call him Westie. She turned to Meredith with a forced grin. "He's not my viscount, yet."

"Ah, Miss Hewett. At last I've found you."

Julia's cheeks heated as Westie materialized out of the crowd. Had he heard any of that? His pleasant smile would suggest otherwise. His navy coat and carefully tied cravat were spotless, and he carried himself with his usual ease. Nothing to Tanner's powerful stance, but still.

"Thank you for inviting me," Westie said, blue eyes sparkling. "This is fascinating."

"I'm so glad you could join us," Julia told him. "It is the future of the empire, my father tells me. Have you met Lady Belfort?"

He had not, so introductions were quickly exchanged. He managed to ignore Tanner.

"I understand we may have the pleasure of your company at Rose Hill, my lord," Meredith ventured.

"Ah, yes," Westie said. "I received your kind invitation

to visit your friends, Miss Hewett. Nothing would make me happier. Say, tomorrow?"

"Tomorrow?" Julia blinked. "You are willing to come out from London two days in a row?"

"Such devotion," Daring agreed.

She thought Tanner rolled his eyes.

"Actually, I'm staying in the area with my cousin, Lady Alldene." He nodded to where a woman draped in a long, black veil stood, each hand gripping that of a boy, with a little girl clinging to her widow's weeds. The children seemed as fascinated as Westie with the train.

"Yes, I heard about the earl's death last year," Julia said. "Perhaps I should offer my condolences."

"Allow me to introduce you," Westie replied. "If you will excuse us, Lady Belfort."

Meredith inclined her head.

Westie went to put his hand on Julia's elbow and started, then glowered at Tanner, whose fingers were already firmly planted.

"This way, my dear," Tanner said smoothly, helping her through the crowd.

Through the black lace veil, Julia could just make out the countess's fair hair and elegant features. Her two sons had light brown hair that was already curling from the steam and inquisitive blue eyes, where her daughter, a few years younger, was dark-haired and dark-eyed, likely favoring her father, who had invested in the railway.

"Thea," Westie said, stepping in front of Tanner, "allow me to present a dear friend of mine, Miss Julia Hewett. Her father is the clever fellow behind this demonstration."

"And Mr. Tanner," Julia put in.

"Miss Hewett, Mr. Tanner," the countess said in a calm, collected voice. Through the veil, sharp blue eyes regarded her. "These are my sons, Lord Shaw and James, and my daughter, Lady Audra."

"Does your father really drive the train?" the younger boy asked. Julia would have guessed him about eight and his brother about a year or so older.

"No, he pulls it with his carriage," his brother gibed.

"My father had the idea for the railway," Julia explained to them with a smile. "He hired Mr. Stephenson to build the engine and Mr. Winston there to lay the tracks. Mr. Churchman will actually drive the engine."

"I wish I could drive the engine," the little girl said with a sigh, twining one raven curl around her finger.

Westie laughed. "Well, that would be interesting. But pretty young ladies have no need to drive great dirty engines."

That sounded rather dismissive. Julia's temper raised its head. "Although they certainly could if they wanted," she said as the little girl frowned at him.

Her mother smiled at her. "Well said, Miss Hewett. I always applaud initiative and innovation from anyone."

Westie's handsome face darkened, but he inclined his head graciously.

"Ladies and gentlemen!" Her father's voice boomed over the crowd, and all heads turned in his direction. "Thank you for coming to see the fruition of months of hard work and years of planning. This is only the second of Mr. Stephenson's engines to make its debut, with the other engine at Darrington, so we're in rare company indeed. I'd like to thank Mr. Winston and Mr. Churchman for their efforts and recognize all the men who made this day possible."

Everyone applauded, and the two men near the front of the group beamed around.

"If our guests would take their seats," her father continued, "we'll see what these wizards of industry have accomplished."

The countess gathered her children closer and shepherded them up into the car.

Westie looked to Julia, but all she could do was offer him a smile before allowing Tanner to escort her.

Westie gallantly gave his arm to Daring and they fell in behind her and Tanner as they all headed for the open car.

The cars had been designed like great boxes on iron wheels. They would hold all manner of goods being shipped from Surrey into London and the London docks out to Surrey. The car for their ride had been fitted with narrow benches that could hold no more than three on either side of a center aisle. Tanner allowed Daring to enter one of the rows first, then intercepted Westie before he could be seated. For a moment, the two glared at each other.

Julia took the initiative. "As our guest, you should sit next to my father, my lord. I'm sure you and he have much to discuss."

Westie favored her with a tight smile. "As you wish, Miss Hewett." With one more pointed look to Tanner, he settled himself across the aisle. At least her father would be too busy to notice who was beside him until the train started moving. She could only hope her viscount would make good use of the opportunity and impress her father.

Once everyone was settled, her father called the all clear to the engineer at the front. She couldn't see what he or the two workers were doing over the pile of coal between her and them, but the steam poured from the stack and the car gave a jerk. Her father dropped down onto the bench, and she clutched at Tanner to keep from tipping forward.

He put his arm about her shoulders and kept her steady.

The great wheels began to turn, the car to move forward. Slow, fast, faster, until the steam was streaming past over their heads and the wind was nipping at her cheeks. She heard a cry from one of the gentlemen as his top hat was blown clear off. She should be looking at

Westie and her father to see how they were getting along, but she couldn't seem to take her eyes off the swiftly passing countryside.

"How fast does this engine go?" Tanner asked over the rattle of the car.

"Father said fifteen miles per hour," she called back, one hand on her bonnet.

It felt as if they were flying. Tanner let out a whoop, and she laughed at the sheer joy of it. Around them, others exclaimed or cheered. Her father glanced back at his guests with a grin.

The two workers clambered over the dwindling pile of coal to take positions at the front of the car.

"Stay in your seats," the taller commanded, pistol in one hand. "This is a robbery. Hand over your valuables, and no one gets hurt."

"And if you don't hand them over," the shorter said, "she's the first one we'll shoot."

He aimed his pistol directly at Julia.

Tanner stood and put himself in front of Julia only to find that Mrs. Daring had already yanked her flat onto the bench. Across the aisle and out of the corner of his eye, he saw Keller sheltering Miss Bee. Roth, who had been sitting on the outside of a row near the countess, shifted his body into a ready position. His dark head went down and up as his gaze caught Tanner's. Ready, as always, for a fight.

But Tanner would do nothing that might jeopardize Julia's life.

"I'll keep her safe," Mrs. Daring murmured. "Stop them."

He wasn't sure why the word of an elderly, diminutive woman would sway his judgment, but he believed her.

After his brash statement that she would be shot first

if anyone misbehaved, the shorter robber was making his way down the aisle, focused on the south side while his friend worked the north. Caps out, they loomed over the guests, who fumbled for watches, coin purses, and jewelry. The clack of the wheels and rumble of the engine dominated.

Tanner caught Roth's gaze again. His colleague planted both feet firmly in the aisle.

Between Tanner and the robbers, Lord Westerbrook rose to his feet, hands held out in supplication. "Gentlemen, gentlemen. What sort of villain threatens a lady? If you must have a target, use me."

Hewett stared at him. So did Julia, mouth agape and brows going up in evident admiration. Did the man think he could truly protect her with appeasement?

But the robber who had threatened Julia apparently thought so, for he lowered his pistol. "You're right, my lord. My own mother would be ashamed of me."

His friend shoved his cap at Lady Belfort. "Me mum's dead and wouldn't give a care one way or the other. I'll be taking that ring, milady."

"*Jetz!*" Roth cried in the German the guards all spoke a moment before his hand seized the pistol.

The taller robber swiveled toward Roth and aimed. Tanner didn't stop to think. He lunged forward, grasped the fellow's shoulders from behind, and planted his boot in the robber's knee. He crumbled. Tanner shoved him to the floor of the car and kept him there.

"What are you doing!" the viscount cried. "I had the matter in hand!"

Tanner glanced up to make sure Roth had the second robber confined. The other Imperial Guardsman had forced his target to the ground as well and was wrenching the gun from his hand. Tanner did the same. His blood roared in his ears. His muscles were taut as bowstrings. But at least Julia was safe.

Her father jumped to his feet. "Ho!" he shouted in the direction of the engine. "Stop the train! Now!"

CHAPTER FOURTEEN

B RAKES SQUEALING, ENGINE coughing, the train slowed, then stopped, rocking everyone forward and back. Tanner widened his stance to remain on his feet even as Julia sat upright and brushed off her pelisse. Keller took a sobbing Miss Bee in his arms. Lord Westerbrook looked daggers at Tanner, but Julia gave him two thumbs up and a grin. Mrs. Daring nodded her thanks.

The head of the engineer poked up above the coal pile that separated them. "Where are my shovelers? What's happened?"

"There's been a robbery," Hewett told him. "Or at least there would have been if not for the valiant efforts of the Imperial Guards. It seems your lads are criminals." He glanced to Tanner. "You have them secure now?"

Roth hauled his robber to his feet and gave him a shake. "He'll cause no more trouble."

"This one either," Tanner said, scowling at the fellow as he pulled him up as well.

"Good lads." Hewett looked back to his engineer, who was goggling. "Do we have enough coal in the fire to take us to the station, Mr. Churchman?"

Churchman gathered himself and stood taller. "Aye, sir."

"Then off you go. We'll escort these fellows to the Duke of Wey. He can decide whether to hold them over for the assizes."

Applause rang out from the other guests as the robbers

hung their heads. Keller came to take Tanner's prisoner from him, and the other two guards escorted the pair to the back of the car. Neither robber looked as if he had much fight left in him.

Tanner bent and picked up first the one and then the other cap that had fallen and handed them to Mr. Bee.

"Would you see these returned to the rightful owners, sir?"

"With pleasure," he said, rising as his youngest gazed at Tanner in obvious awe.

He walked back up the aisle to join Julia.

"Thank you," she murmured as he dropped down beside her. "That was amazing."

He shrugged, though his pulse would not slow. "All part of my job."

He felt the loss of her smile as she directed it toward Lord Westerbrook, who had somehow managed to squeeze onto the bench behind her. "And thank you, my lord. That was very brave of you to confront them unarmed."

"And ill-witted," Mrs. Daring muttered. Tanner hid a smile.

"Well, I never could stand a man who bullies women," Lord Westerbrook said. He leaned forward, closing the distance between them. "I do hope you know you can count on me, dear Julia."

Her father came toward them and jerked a thumb back. "Move. Now. I need to speak with my daughter privately."

The viscount's jaw tightened, but he sat upright and looked away as if he couldn't care less. Tanner dropped back beside Lord Westerbrook to give his employer pride of place.

Everyone braced themselves as the engine started forward again.

He wasn't certain what Julia's father was saying to her

under the chug of the engine, but what he could see of her cheek reddened with every word. Worse, Lord Westerbrook had leaned forward on his seat again, head tipped, as if trying to hear every word.

Tanner dropped his heel down on the fellow's instep and had the satisfaction of hearing a muffled oath.

"Crowded," Tanner commented, shifting on the bench.

"It certainly is," Westerbrook drawled.

The engine brought them in to the platform at Moseley with no further mishaps. Many of the guests must have sent their carriages ahead, for a string of coaches was waiting beside the warehouses. Tanner escorted Julia and Mrs. Daring from the car. He could feel Westerbrook fuming behind them.

He kept his gaze moving, from the solid walls of the wooden warehouses to the narrow lanes that ran between them, but aside from a worker or two hurrying about his business, he saw nothing of concern. Even the rain was holding off, the clouds flying across the sky as if they hoped to follow the new engine on its course.

"Mr. Tanner."

He turned to find the countess and her children approaching. "Your ladyship," he said with a bow.

"That was very well done, sir," she said, and both her sons were watching him wide-eyed, as if he'd sprouted wings. "If you ever have need of a position, please let me know."

"What an excellent suggestion," Lord Westerbrook all but purred. "I'm sure you could find some menial task that needs his sort of brawn around your castle, Thea."

The veil hid much of her expression, but her shoulders tightened. "I have the utmost respect for Mr. Tanner. He would be a most welcome addition to our household."

Tanner shook his head. "Thank you, but I am content where I am, for now, Lady Alldene."

Lady Belfort, who was passing, paused beside them.

"If you are seeking someone of Mr. Tanner's skills, Lady Alldene, I'd be more than happy to speak to you about one of the other guards. They have been lauded by the Duke and Duchess of Wey."

"And Lord and Lady Kendall, I believe," the countess said, voice lightening. "I have greatly enjoyed becoming better acquainted with Ivy. She thinks the world of you."

"And I of her," Lady Belfort assured her. "Allow me to entertain you and your children at Rose Hill at your convenience." Her smile included the two sons and the daughter.

"You might want to rethink that invitation, dear lady," Lord Westerbrook put in. "These two can be a bit mischievous and require a firm hand." He reached out to ruffle the hair of the oldest boy, who ducked away from him and favored him with a frown.

"Perhaps we could speak now," the countess said. "If you would excuse me a moment, Westerbrook. I know these domestic issues bore you."

Lady Belfort stepped aside with Lady Alldene and the children. The little girl glanced back at Tanner and waved.

"You didn't mention Lady Belfort was friends with the Marquess of Kendall," Lord Westerbrook said to Julia. Was that worry in his voice? Why?

"The Marquess of Kendall, the Duke of Wey, the Earl of Carrolton, Sir Harold Orwell, Viscount Worthington, Sir Matthew Bateman, and Lord Ashforde," Mrs. Daring supplied helpfully.

"Not to mention King Frederick and Crown Prince Otto Leopold, as well as Count Montalban of the kingdom of Batavaria," Tanner said, watching the fellow.

"All of whom were matched by Lady Belfort's cat, if the stories are true," Julia said. "Except for the king, of course."

Westerbrook's smile lacked its usual gleam. "Tomorrow should be quite interesting, then."

"I can hardly wait," Julia agreed.

Neither could Tanner.

Meredith eyed Lady Alldene as she and her children reached the edge of the platform. The countess's estate lay to the southwest, beyond Meredith's usual sphere of influence, but she had sent a condolence card on the death of the lady's husband last year. The veil hid much, but it seemed to her there was tension in those slender shoulders. Grief, or something more? Oh, if only she had Fortune with her!

Lady Alldene lay a hand on her oldest son's shoulder. "Shaw, would you make sure your brother and sister reach the coach? I'll join you shortly."

The boy glanced curiously at Meredith, then nodded and began chivvying his siblings toward a waiting coach lacquered in a deep blue with silver appointments.

"Forgive me," Lady Alldene said, facing Meredith at last. "While I would love to discuss the possibility of having one of the Imperial Guards join our household as a tutor for my sons, there is a more pressing matter. Am I right in assuming that you and Miss Hewett are good friends?"

"I believe Julia would agree that we are," Meredith told her, mystified.

Lady Alldene hesitated. Others were streaming past for their carriages, voices raised in conversation. The robbery was mentioned as often as the engine. Meredith felt for John Hewett. To have created such a marvelous event only to have it eclipsed by skullduggery!

As if making a decision, Lady Alldene took a step closer and lowered her voice. "I strongly suggest that you encourage your friend to look more closely at Lord Westerbrook before committing herself to him. He is my husband's cousin and the guardian of my children, but I have not found him to be a pleasant fellow."

Interesting. "Then I'm even more pleased that he's coming to see us tomorrow," Meredith said.

It was not what the countess had expected, for she stiffened. "You must have noticed that he attempts to charm in public. I can assure you he can be quite different in private."

Meredith put a hand on her arm. "Never fear, Lady Alldene. I would not allow anyone I cared about to marry a scoundrel. I am merely confident we can get his lordship to show his true colors. And I look forward to having you and your children visit, so we can continue discussing how else the Imperial Guards might be of service."

What a day! The excitement of the ride, the danger of the robbery, and a royal scold from her father for praising Westie because he'd attempted to diffuse the situation! Julia barely managed to settle into her seat in the carriage as it headed for home.

Her father had decided to stay behind and see the robbers escorted to the duke personally.

"And I'll make sure they're questioned as to why they decided to single Julia out," she'd overheard him tell Tanner before they'd left. "You make sure she gets home safely."

"You have my word," Tanner had promised him before clapping his fist to his chest.

Westie had also wanted to escort her home. "What if these miscreants had friends?" he'd asked as he'd stood beside her carriage, gazing up at her longingly as she looked down from the open window.

"Miscreants seldom have friends," Daring had murmured from inside the coach. "That's why they became miscreants."

While Tanner had climbed up with Mr. Towser, Julia

had focused on the man below her. Speckles of coal dust had peppered his top hat, and his handsome face had paled, as if leaving her was simply too much to bear.

"Much as I would adore your company," she'd told him, "Father has probably had enough for today. And we will see each other tomorrow at Rose Hill." She'd reached out, and he'd taken her hand and pressed a kiss against her fingers.

She rubbed at her hand now as the carriage sped toward Weyton with Tanner on the roof with the coachman. She had imagined what it might feel like to have Westie kiss her. Surely there would be a thrill, almost as good as when the engine had reached top speed. But she'd only wanted to tug her fingers out of his grip before his lips had even touched them. And his kiss had left her feeling almost queasy, quite unlike the kiss of a certain russet-haired bodyguard.

She was suddenly very glad Tanner was on the roof instead of in the carriage with her!

He stayed close again that afternoon, sharing his impressions from the wall as she and Daring discussed the attempted robbery. Julia finally heard the door an hour before they usually ate dinner and came out of the library to meet her father, Tanner and Daring at her back.

"What did they say?" she asked as Garrison took her father's coat.

He didn't need to ask who she meant. "Kept their mouths shut on the way to the castle," he said with a wrinkle of his nose that set his mustache to twitching. "Unfortunately, another fellow with a rifle met us and liberated them before we could turn them over to the duke."

"What!" Julia cried.

Tanner stepped forward. "Keller? Roth?"

"Focused on protecting me," her father admitted, rubbing the back of his neck with one hand. "While

I appreciate the gesture, I was sorry to see the villains escape."

"So am I," Julia assured him. "But I think the Imperial Guards made the right choice."

He came to enfold her in a hug, big arms tight around her. "Those might not have been highwaymen, as that note threatened, but I still could have lost you today, my girl. You're all I have." His normally strong voice faltered.

Julia pressed her face into the warmth of his jacket, the scent of his pipe tobacco tickling her nose. "I'm not going anywhere."

"Good," he said, releasing her. "For the next few days, I think."

She started. "No, Father, that's not what I meant! I have a very important appointment at Rose Hill tomorrow."

He sighed. "Well, you ought to be safe there, so long as Keller and Roth are in residence."

"They are," Tanner allowed, but she could see by the set of his jaw that the robbers' escape troubled him as much as it did her.

Her father seemed to have recovered, for he clapped his hands together. "That's settled, then. Nothing like a bit of excitement to give a man an appetite. Who's ready for dinner?"

Garrison immediately signaled the footman, who took off for the kitchen, likely to warn Mrs. Cheevers that her food would be wanted sooner than expected.

"So, what did you think of my engine?" her father asked, linking arms with her.

"It did very well," Julia allowed as they ambled toward the dining room, Tanner and Daring following. "I couldn't believe how fast it flew."

"Like a falcon after prey," her father agreed.

"And then the robbery," Daring put in. "I cannot understand how Mr. Churchman would hire robbers as workers."

"That was badly done," her father admitted as they reached the double doors. "I'll be expecting a better accounting in future, I can promise you."

"I still say Lord Westerbrook was quite brave to stand up to them," Julia ventured with a glance at her father.

He pulled away and marched toward his chair at the head of the table. "Fool! He could have gotten himself and you killed. I was just glad the guards were along."

Truth be told, so was she. "Yes, Mr. Tanner, Mr. Keller, and Mr. Roth were the heroes of the day," she acknowledged as Tanner sat across from her. "I've already thanked you once, but I thank you again, sir."

He inclined his head. "As I told you, it was only my duty."

"And a nicely executed duty it was too," her father said as Garrison came forward with the wine. "Remind me to give you a raise, my lad."

Something crossed Tanner's face, and it wasn't delight at the idea of more income. It was almost as if he didn't think he'd earned it.

After the day they'd had, the evening was entirely too quiet, especially given Julia's hopes for the morrow. It was all she could do to stay at Hewett House the next morning long enough to be proper before setting out for Rose Hill. She wore her spruce-colored gown with the ruff at the throat and her bonnet with the peacock feathers. She had suggested to Tanner he might have the day off, but he was adamant about coming.

"A dedication to duty is admirable," Daring said as she took her seat beside Julia for the ride.

"I suppose so," Julia said.

"I certainly would not have survived this long without it," Daring reminded her.

She smiled. "I know I can be a sad trial. Thank you for putting up with my mad starts."

"They certainly make life interesting," Daring said.

They spoke of their upcoming plans to collect coats and blankets for the poor, as they had every winter for the last five years, but the closer they drew to Rose Hill, the more Julia's stomach tightened. Why was she so nervous? Fortune adored her, and she was sure to approve of Westie. Then again, Fortune had been contrary of late. What if she approved of neither of them!

Tanner jumped down from the bench and opened the coach door for her before the footman could.

"No sign of trouble on the road," he reported as if he had expected to find marauders around every bend. Then again, after yesterday…

"You would probably be fine riding inside with us," Julia suggested as they headed for the door.

"Easier to spot a problem from outside in daylight," he told her. Then he smiled at Mr. Cowls in the open doorway.

The butler ushered them into the house and took their wraps. "Miss Hewett, Mrs. Daring, Mr. Tanner, welcome back. Her ladyship is expecting you."

They found Meredith waiting in the upstairs withdrawing room, Fortune at her feet. Julia and Daring sat, but the cat immediately went to Tanner, who was standing by one of the walls. Instead of winding around his boots, she attacked one tassel. Tanner took a step back to remove the bits of leather from her reach. Chin up, she stalked off toward the sofa.

"Don't leave!" Julia called after her. "You're the first actress of this drama."

Fortune paused to glance back over her shoulder at Julia, copper-colored eyes sparkling, as if she knew exactly what she was doing. Then she slipped out of sight behind the sofa.

Julia shook her head. "I am obviously doing something wrong."

"She keeps her own counsel," Meredith said with a

smile. "But I'm certain she'll want to meet your viscount. Do we expect him soon?"

As if in answer to her question, a knock sounded on the door downstairs. Julia tensed.

"Lord Westerbrook to see Lady Belfort." The polished voice sent a shiver through her.

"You are expected, my lord," Cowls replied, but his voice was not nearly as welcoming as it had been to Julia.

A moment more, and her intended appeared in the doorway. He'd chosen a caramel-colored coat fitted to his frame, and his cravat was a masterpiece of cascading folds. She beamed as he strolled into the room and bowed over Meredith's hand before greeting the others, even Tanner.

"How nice of you to join us," Meredith said with a glance at the spot on the sofa next to her.

Westie flipped up his tails and moved to sit, but he hadn't even reached the sofa before he sneezed.

"I do beg your pardon," he said, perching beside her. "And how are you after our excitement of yesterday?"

"Quite well," Meredith said. "Though I suspect Julia was the more troubled by the event."

A paw snaked out from one side of the sofa and poked at Westie's boot.

"It was all over so quickly," Julia said, angling her head to catch sight of the cat. "I barely had time to..."

Westie sneezed again, and Fortune's paw disappeared. He held up one hand and reached for a handkerchief in his pocket with the other.

Julia leaned forward. "Are you well, my lord?"

He waved the handkerchief. "Fine, fine, my dear. I'm not sure what came over me. You were say—achoo!"

From his spot along the wall, Tanner arched a brow as sneezes shot through the air.

Julia put a hand to her chest to stop the thudding of her heart. "Perhaps we should send for the physician."

Westie rose, limbs trembling. "Please do not—

achoo!—trouble yourself on—achoo!—my account, Miss—achoo!—Hewett. I beg your pardon, Lady Belfort. Perhaps we could visit another day. Achoo!"

Head bowed over his handkerchief, he quit the room.

"How very disappointing," Daring said in the silence that followed.

Fortune sashayed out from behind the sofa and onto the carpet, pausing for a leisurely stretch that arched her back.

"There you are!" Julia cried. "I was counting on you!"

Fortune regarded her archly, then strolled to the landing, where she peered down at the fleeing viscount. Her tail lashed back and forth, back and forth.

"As if she's spotted a rat and hoped to pounce," Meredith murmured, watching her pet.

"Oh, surely not!" Julia said. "She never had a chance to meet him. Very likely his sneezes made her jittery."

"Perhaps," her friend acknowledged. "But I very much fear, Julia, that Lord Westerbrook is not all that he seems."

CHAPTER FIFTEEN

JULIA SETTLED ONTO the seat next to Daring as the carriage started for home. Fortune had not appreciated Lord Westerbrook, and Meredith had confided that even his cousin, Lady Alldene, had misgivings about him. Was his character truly so abhorrent? Her spirits should be plummeting.

Instead, she felt a lightening, a relief. Why?

"I do hope Lord Westerbrook's illness isn't contagious," Daring mused, tugging her shawl a little closer. "My nose is already itching."

Julia glanced at her. Daring's button nose looked no different than usual. "Your nose isn't red, and neither are your eyes. Perhaps he has an aversion to cats."

She heaved one of her sighs. "A terrible affliction. I am rather partial to feline companions."

Julia nudged her. "I far prefer the two-legged variety."

"For now, dear," Daring said with a smile. "But you might enjoy the company of a pet after you've wed."

"As I hope to travel, I'm not sure that would be wise," Julia told her as the carriage bowled through Weyton. "I could hardly take my pet with me; the poor thing would be forever left behind. That's no way to treat an animal."

"Perhaps Lord Westerbrook would remain behind so as to provide a stabilizing influence in your pet's life," Daring suggested.

Julia raised her brows. "Leave my husband behind? Do you think Lord Westerbrook so timid?"

"Not timid," Daring hazarded, smoothing down her pelisse. "But rather set in his ways, particularly as to the role of women, especially ones above a certain age." She tugged on her shawl again.

Her temper began bubbling. "Was he rude to you? I will not countenance it."

Daring reached out to pat her hand. "You needn't trouble yourself on my account. I can protect myself." As if to prove otherwise, she sneezed.

Perhaps Lord Westerbrook *had* been contagious!

Tanner was climbing down from the bench as the footman opened the door for Julia and Daring, but she made sure to escort her companion into the house, Tanner at their heels.

"Is everything all right?" he asked as if he'd noticed her quickened steps.

Daring sneezed again. "Pardon me, I'm sure."

Tanner took a step back. So did Garrison, and his long nose turned up.

"I'll be down shortly," Julia told Tanner before taking Daring straight to her room. She made sure her companion was settled with a good book to read and handkerchiefs and hot tea at her elbow. As she left the room, she twitched her nose, but felt not the slightest urge to sneeze. Odd.

The corridor seemed wide, cool, and silent as she wandered toward the stairs. Easy for thoughts to creep up on her. And rather logical that those thoughts turned to Lord Westerbrook.

She had initially been attracted to him because he was handsome and charming, and he didn't seem to be after her fortune. She was confident in her appearance and character, but she was all too aware that some men saw those as only the icing on the cake of her considerable inheritance. He had seemed to genuinely appreciate her. He certainly had many titled and powerful friends, which should have endeared him to her father but clearly hadn't.

But she had to own that, the more they had become acquainted, the less she had found to admire. His sense of humor was a bit lacking. He didn't always see the wit in a situation. And he was rather set in his ways, as Daring had said. He could well take exception to her hopes of traveling and insist that she follow a more traditional path of supervising his household and bearing his children. And though yesterday he had shown a bravery she would not have expected, he had also shown a naïve presumption that a mere word from him would stop the robbers.

Perhaps it was time she faced the fact that he wasn't the man for her. Which meant another Season next spring, and another year she would have to hold off on her dreams of traveling.

A sigh very much like Daring's leaked out as she started down the stairs, and she gripped the polished rosewood banister overly hard. Was it too much to ask to find a groom of good character and wit, with an interest in travel, who could be honest with her and overlook her fortune?

"Is Mrs. Daring all right?" Tanner asked.

She stepped down into the entry hall to find him waiting by the door of her father's study. The footman on duty in the entry hall kept his face forward, but his gaze darted to her as she approached Tanner.

"I suspect we won't know until morning. Regardless, I'm sure she appreciated a little time to herself."

"I noticed she does not take a half-day off," he said, falling into step beside her as she headed for the library.

Julia cocked her head. "Do you know, I never thought to ask! Daring has always been at my side since my mother died when I was twelve." She straightened as they entered the book-filled room. "How thoughtless of me! I will ask her tomorrow which day she'd like off. Goodness knows, she's earned quite a few."

She glanced at Tanner as she went to sit near the hearth. One of the footmen had kindled a fire, and she hugged its warmth close. Rain hit the window, the patter muffled by the thick draperies.

"You haven't taken a day off either," she reminded him, spreading her skirts. "Do I need to speak to Father?"

He put his back to one of the bookcases. "As your bodyguard, I would only take time off if relieved of duty. There is no other, except your father, to relieve me. And a fiancé wouldn't be given time off."

"There is that." She eyed him. "A fiancé wouldn't stand around watching either, you know."

"He would if he thought his lady in danger."

She rolled her head back. "Danger? Tanner, I'm in one of the least assailable rooms in my home. What danger could find me here?"

"Someone inserted those notes into the post," he pointed out. "It could have been one of your servants."

She snapped her head upright so quickly, she earned herself a crick. "Nonsense," she said, rubbing the spot with one hand. "They've all been with us since I was a child."

"Plenty of time to suffer under grievances," he said.

"Father may be gruff, but he pays quite well, I'm told. He remembers what it was like having nothing."

He nodded. "You mentioned that he started from humble beginnings."

"Orphan in a coal mine," she confirmed. "He was what they call a pit boy—sent down into tight spaces the men couldn't reach, spending his time fetching and carrying otherwise. It sounds like a dark, dank existence."

"Roth had a similar experience, only in the silver mines of Batavaria," Tanner said. "It is a hard life."

"So Father says. But he was given the right to bring out whatever pieces of coal he could fit in his pockets. Instead of using that coal in his own little hovel, he sold it to buy a coat with bigger pockets."

He chuckled. "Clever lad."

"He was like that his whole life," Julia said, settling deeper into the chair, "trading comfort today for a better future. I suspect that's why he keeps holding out for a duke for me. He doesn't mind me going through the trouble of endless Seasons in London, so long as there are a title and a manor at the end."

"Wealth and position," he said, sticking out his lower lip. "Not bad goals."

The memory of how those lips had felt against hers intruded, warmer than the fire beside her. She tore her gaze away.

"Knowledge and experience are better goals," she countered. "I'm well aware my fortune could give me such opportunities, if I had a husband at my side." Her neck twinged again, and she wiggled her shoulders. "Must you stand there, Tanner? It would be easier to have a conversation if you sat."

His mouth quirked. "You don't seem to have any trouble carrying on a conversation in any position."

She rose. "If you are trying to tell me I talk too much, you're too late. Father and Daring have been suggesting it for years." She strolled closer. "But the conversation needn't be about me or my family. With Daring ill, we have the entire afternoon open before us. I'd be delighted to speak about what interests you." She stopped in front of him and met those dark eyes.

"So, I would very much like to know: what interests you, Tanner?"

With her standing there, gaze turned up to his, eyes intent, only one word popped into his mind.

You.

Not what a bodyguard should say to his charge.

"Have we nothing else planned?" he asked.

Her face fell, as if he had disappointed her, and she resumed her pacing. Had she no idea the movement called attention to her curves? He should direct his gaze elsewhere, but the sway of those skirts was mesmerizing.

"Oh, come now," she teased, glancing over her shoulder at him, "you must have other interests. What of travel, adventure?"

How had she known? He didn't recall speaking of his goals in her presence. "I have traveled with the king, but I would like to do more. I even asked Lord Worthington whether he and his wife needed someone with my skills. Sadly, he did not."

She turned in a swirl of wool and ambled back toward him. "I always thought this job was too tame for you. What are you looking for? Intrigue? Danger?" Her brows went up. "Espionage?"

She was right in front of him again, and he caught the scent of lilacs. Immediately, he was standing at the foot of the Batavarian mountains, gazing up at the sky above the peaks and longing to see what was on the other side.

"My father was one of Batavaria's greatest heroes," he told her. "Every man, woman, and child knew his name. Even though I distinguished myself during the war with Napoleon, I always wondered if I was chosen to join the Imperial Guards because of him."

She nodded. "The name of John Hewett is becoming known as well. Many judge me, one way or the other, because of him."

Perhaps she'd understand. "My father did many praiseworthy things, things I am unlikely to be called upon to do. But he never stepped more than fifty miles from where he was born. He conquered Batavaria. I want to conquer the world."

She grinned. "Done. I'll get Lord Westerbrook to hire you as our bodyguard when we travel."

The winter wind blew from his father's mountains and swept between them as she stepped back, blinking.

"Then you're still considering accepting him," Tanner said, voice coming out as heavy as he felt.

"No, I…" She set about pacing again, as if now trying to outrun her own thoughts. "That is, I am not well pleased with him at the moment. I do not wish to discuss it. You wanted to talk of plans. Let us talk of plans."

She made it sound as if he wanted to converse about the delights of toe fungus.

He found himself smiling, but more from the sheer relief that she might have decided to throw off the fool. "You don't like planning."

"I plan!" she insisted, turning past the hearth. "I'll have you know that Daring and I manage the collection of warm coats and blankets for the poor among us every year before winter comes. We've already begun discussing who we will approach this year."

"Commendable," he said.

She paused to eye him a moment, as if trying to hear sarcasm under the word. Then she turned and set off toward the hearth again. "Of course, Christmas is coming." She stopped in front of the fire, where the light set red flames dancing in her hair, and glanced his way again. "I suppose I should think of a gift for you. Some would expect it of a fiancée."

Something poked into his back, and he took a step away from the bookcase. Still the feeling persisted. He should have known it wasn't physical. The dishonesty between them rankled more each day. He'd told her father he intended to explain the situation at the first opportunity, and he'd only tried once. And he'd thought *her* mercurial!

"About our so-called engagement," he started.

"Tanner!"

The word barked from the doorway, and he and Julia both looked that direction. Her father stood there, glowering.

"Sir," Tanner said, head up.

"My study. Now." Hewett turned and stalked out.

Julia ran to seize Tanner's arm before he could follow, eyes wide in a face that was paling. "What have you done?"

"Nothing except my job," Tanner assured her. He put his hand over hers. "Whatever it is, I won't let anything harm you, Julia."

She relaxed, smile soft and hopeful. "I know that. But I'm finding it just as difficult to think of anyone hurting *you*."

And there came that feeling again—to hold her, to kiss her, to promise her he'd never leave her side. But bodyguards and pretend fiancés did not have the option of acting on those feelings.

He pulled away. "I should do as he bids. I'll return as soon as I can."

She nodded, and he left her, her touch still warm upon his arm.

Her father was standing by the fire in his study. The light flickered in his hair as well, but the effect wasn't nearly as charming, especially with the glower still stamped on his face.

Tanner came to a stop in front of him and clapped his fist to his chest. "Your servant, sir."

"And you'd better remember that," Hewett said, eyes narrowing. "Am I wrong, or were you about to tell my daughter everything?"

Tanner kept his head up and his voice level. "I was clear that I intended to explain at the right moment. Today seemed right."

"Wrong," he snapped. "She was nearly shot yesterday. You protected her, and for that, I will always be grateful. But do you think she'd have a similar confidence in your protection if she learned you were lying to her?"

Possibly not, and that trust was critical to keeping a client safe. Why had he agreed to something that might jeopardize that? Had he been so determined to remain at her side even then? As it was, when he considered his future, he no longer thought only of his hopes, but hers.

"I should never have consented," Tanner said. "I can only hope she'll forgive me."

Hewett shook his head, and his spirits sank further. "I wouldn't be so sure about that." He went to sit in one of the chairs and motioned Tanner into the other. He had to force himself down.

"There's another reason I'd prefer you hold off on telling her the truth," her father explained. "I can see that she's thinking things through, as I'd hoped. I expect her to throw off the viscount shortly. If you tell her before then, you could push her right into his arms."

Hewett was right. She'd just admitted she wasn't pleased with the fellow. Would it hurt so very much to wait a few more days? The damage couldn't be any worse.

"Very well," Tanner said. "I will honor your wishes."

"Good lad." He leaned back. "In the meantime, don't get comfortable in my daughter's presence. You're a fine fellow, but you're no duke or prince." He chuckled.

Tanner couldn't find the humor in it. He had been serving dukes and princes most of his life. They were little different from other men. Those who took their roles seriously, like Prince Otto Leopold and the Duke of Wey, had been tempered by the trust and expectations placed on them. Others saw their positions of power merely as tools to force others to their desires.

"Your daughter could do better than many princes and dukes I have met," he said.

Her father smiled. "I couldn't agree more. She could do far better than a soldier with no home or family name, either."

The truth snapped at him like a dog on a chain. "Agreed," he gritted out.

Hewett nodded. "I'm glad we could come to a consensus. Just remember, I never intended this engagement to be real."

Neither had he, only now it felt entirely too real. And he wasn't sure what to do about it.

CHAPTER SIXTEEN

JULIA HAD YANKED every book from the shelf and pressed her ear to the paneling, but the conversation between her father and Tanner had been much quieter than usual, and she had heard little.

Her father had been in a towering mood when he'd found them in the library. She'd recognized the color in his cheeks, the bristle of his mustache. What would she do if he discharged Tanner? She couldn't imagine going back to life without him at her side. He'd become like Daring, always there, always a comfort, someone she could rely on.

And perhaps more.

By the time he reappeared in the doorway, she had replaced all the books and was standing beside them, watching for him. His face was as smooth as the rosewood banister, and he held himself nearly as stiff.

Her breath caught. "Did he sack you?"

His brows went up. "No. I have done nothing wrong."

"Oh, I'm so glad," she said, breath whooshing out of her. Aware of how giddy she sounded, she put on a smile. "After all, what would I do without my bodyguard fiancé?"

He did not react to her tease, merely going to take up his spot along the bookshelf.

Julia wandered over to a chair and allowed herself to sit. "Has he received another note, then?"

"He did not say," he replied, gazing off across the room as if one of the other bookcases had evil plans. "But if there had been a new threat, he would have told me."

Possibly. "Then why was he so intent on speaking with you?"

He was quiet a moment, and her hands started rubbing together in her lap. She forced them apart.

"Your father is concerned about your future," he said. "He wanted to make sure I understood that."

An odd time to state his case, again. But her father was given to mad starts as well. The apple truly didn't fall far from the tree.

A sneeze from the doorway drew both their attention. Daring toddled into the room and took a chair. "Thank you for a quiet moment, my dear," she said with a smile to Julia. "I'm feeling much more the thing. Do we know when dinner is planned?"

Not long afterward, as it turned out. At least Tanner sat at the table. He was not much for conversation, however, and her father's frown aimed his way more than once. Even her companion kept glancing between the three of them, brow puckered.

"Has something happened between you and Mr. Tanner?" Daring asked as they retired from the table and started up the stairs for Julia's suite.

"Not nearly enough," Julia said.

Daring regarded her as they came out on the landing.

"Sorry," Julia said. "Thinking out loud, a habit I need to stop."

Daring waved a hand. "Don't mind me, dear. I seldom listen anyway."

Julia slipped an arm about her waist. "You listen exceptionally well. And I, unfortunately do not. Nor do I think as much as I should. I realized today that you've never had a day off."

"You aren't an onerous chore," Daring said as Julia released her to enter her suite. "And I'm not entirely sure what I'd do with myself if I did have time off."

Julia had hoped Tanner would be in a better frame of mind the next day, but he was already out practicing when she and Daring came down to breakfast, and she only caught a glimpse of him passing the doorway before he joined them later in the library. She and Daring had decided to lay out their plans for the clothing collection. Daring, of course, had thought to save their plans from the previous year. She had the notes spread out on a table she had had Quinn arrange between their chairs while Tanner insisted on bracing one of the bookcases again.

Julia did her best to ignore him, but she couldn't help glancing up from time to time. And each time, his gaze and hers brushed, held, and she lost track entirely of what Daring was saying!

"And is that where you think we should start this year, dear?" her companion asked.

Julia gazed down at the pieces of foolscap. "Yes, of course, with your notes. So wise of you to keep them."

"I believe we established that a quarter hour ago," Daring said. "But I may have misremembered. Age has that effect, I find. What I meant was approaching the Duchess of Wey first seems quite appropriate, with her being the ranking lady in the area. Many will follow her lead."

Tanner shifted, and Julia once more had to tear her gaze away.

"We should add Lady Alldene to the list," she said. "She seemed very nice at the railway opening."

"True," Daring said. "Although she may not be as disposed to help us after that opening endangered her children. But then, she is related to your viscount, so he may have some sway over her."

Julia grimaced. "I no longer consider Lord Westerbrook *my* viscount."

Tanner flashed a grin, then quickly schooled his face. She tried not to grin back. She had no business feeling delighted that he was pleased she no longer considered the viscount a viable candidate for her hand. Not until she'd decided *he* was a viable candidate.

A cough sounded from the doorway.

Julia turned to find Garrison waiting.

"Pardon the interruption, Miss Hewett," he said, inclining his silver-haired head, "but Miss Bee and her sister have come to call. Are you at home?"

She could have done without the younger sister, but she'd told Elspeth to call any time, so she could hardly refuse her now. "Certainly, Garrison. Would you show them to the upstairs withdrawing room? We will join them shortly."

Daring sighed as she gathered up the notes. "So much for planning."

Julia patted her shoulder. "We have time. And the daughters are not nearly as fearsome without their mother."

"So you say," Daring replied.

Julia looked to Tanner, standing so strong and true, his graceful form outlined against the dark of the bookcase. Enough! She stood and shook out her skirts.

"You are supposed to be my fiancé, sir," she announced. "If you intend to be in the same room with our visitors, you will need to take a seat."

His jaw worked a moment. "Perhaps I should wait in the entry hall, then."

If she could not avoid the Bees, neither could he. Julia pressed a hand to the lace at her throat. "And leave me unprotected? What if one of them brought a hat pin? Or worse, a vinaigrette soaked in some foul substance? My very life could be in danger!"

"Garrison will have taken their hats," Tanner said, but she saw a smile hinting.

"And I find vinaigrettes refreshing," Daring put in.

Julia sighed, transferring the back of her hand to her forehead. "Then I suppose I will have to brave their company, alone and friendless."

"Well, not alone," Daring said.

Julia shot her a look.

Tanner laughed, and the sound skipped along her skin, leaving gooseflesh in its wake. "Very well. I will sit with you, but only where I can keep an eye on things."

"I wouldn't have it any other way," Julia assured him, dropping her hand.

He followed them up to the withdrawing room.

The two Bee sisters had taken the sofa, their pink wool skirts a contrast to the green. As Tanner had predicted, Garrison must have taken their hats or bonnets, for their pale blond curls gleamed in the firelight.

Elspeth put out a hand to Julia as she crossed the carpet. "Julia, dear, forgive us for not coming sooner to console you after that horrid robbery."

Her sister sniffed. "Mother said we were safer at home, but I assured her there would be an Imperial Guard to protect us here." She smiled boldly at Tanner.

Julia glanced around. The best seat in the room would be the chair that Daring sometimes took, with its back to the wall and a view out both the window and the door. She chose the chair next to it and had the satisfaction of seeing him sit beside her. Daring selected a chair near Miss Bee the younger on the other side of the sofa.

"I take it your mother was concerned about the event," Julia told her friend.

Elspeth nodded. "She actually took to her bed!"

"First time ever," her sister Angelica confided. "Even Father could not calm her."

"Doctor Shoring prescribed laudanum for the three of us." Elspeth made a face. "I cannot abide it. But I suppose it might have been worth dulling the memory."

Julia hadn't thought the event all that troubling, but then, she'd had Tanner beside her.

"At least no one was hurt," she said.

"No one but those robbers," Angelica said with another smirk to Tanner. Did she not recall he was supposed to be engaged to Julia?

She swished her skirt so that it brushed his boots and leaned slightly closer to him. "I was very glad to have my dear Tanner and the other Imperial Guards with us."

Under the cover of her skirts, Tanner's boot tapped her slipper. What, did he think she was doing it too brown?

"Oh, indeed!" Elspeth agreed. "I don't know what I would have done if Adrian, that is Mr. Keller, hadn't put himself out to protect us."

Daring sent Julia a look. She wasn't the only one to notice the slip. At first names, were they?

"Father is considering hiring him," her sister put in. "So we'll have our own protection too. Especially since Mother heard in Weyton that those robbers escaped." Once again, she looked to Tanner.

Tanner ignored her. Smart fellow.

Elspeth had paled. "Is it difficult, Julia, having the man you love employed by your father?"

Heat pushed up into her cheeks, and this time Julia looked anywhere but at Tanner. "I have not found it particularly onerous."

"Let us speak no more of the incident," Daring said. "I'm sure we're all looking forward to Christmas and Lady Belfort's party. Did I hear that you, Miss Angelica, were planning a new gown?"

Miss Bee the younger tossed her curls. "A lovely

watered silk trimmed in Alençon lace, all the way from France. Nothing but the best, Mother always says. Will you be in attendance, Mr. Tanner?"

Why did she persist? Julia was highly tempted to spill punch at the event on her lovely watered silk!

As if he knew Julia was about to pop, Tanner turned the full of his smile on her instead. "Of course," he said, inclining his head. "I will always go where my love goes."

Was there anything else in the world besides that smile? She seemed to have forgotten.

"How wonderful," Elspeth said with a sigh. "And will Mr. Keller and Mr. Roth also attend?"

He turned to look her way, and Julia blinked as the room came back into focus. Really, she must find some control!

"It will depend on their assignments," Tanner told her friend. "Perhaps you could broach the subject at Sunday services."

Elspeth dropped her gaze and fiddled with the fringe on her sleeve. "Oh, I'm sure Mother would never allow me to be so bold."

Her sister laughed. "Certainly she would. Happily for us both."

They chatted for a while longer before the two sisters made their excuses. Julia walked them to the door, Tanner trailing, but, to her surprise, Angelica pushed in next to her as they started down the stairs behind Daring and Elspeth.

"You can smile all you like," she murmured. "But I know your secret."

Julia kept herself from stumbling with an effort. How could this brash girl have guessed that her engagement to Tanner was a hoax? "I'm sure I have no idea what you're talking about."

Angelica caught her arm to keep her from taking another step, forcing Tanner to stop as well. Her blue eyes were sharp as glass. "You're out to steal my sister. I won't have it. If you keep poaching, I'll make life difficult for you."

"I believe Mr. Garrison is waiting to give you your bonnet, Miss Bee," Tanner said, and his tone brooked no delay.

She offered him a smile that was far removed from her usual look, descended to the entry hall to snatch the bonnet from their butler's hand, and followed her sister out the door.

Daring joined Julia and Tanner at the foot of the stairs. "What was that all about?"

"I have no idea," Julia said, rubbing her arm. "But I begin to wonder whether we've mistaken the person writing the threats after all."

Garrison was already ambling toward the back of the house. Tanner shook his head. "I cannot admire her behavior. But although Miss Bee the younger may have a sting, I suspect it would be easily pulled."

"Not before doing some damage, I warrant," Julia replied, motioning them all to join her again in the library. "She seemed to think I was out to steal her sister's affections from her, which is utter nonsense. A lady may have more than one friend."

"More than one suitor, as well," Daring pointed out. "Although it is generally kinder to let the others free when one has made a decision."

Once more, her cheeks heated. She had made a decision about Lord Westerbrook, but she hadn't told her father or Tanner. Perhaps it was time.

"Excuse me," she said, heading for the door. Tanner made to follow, and she held up her hand. "I'm merely going next door to speak to my father. It will only take a moment."

"Then I will wait for you here," he said.

She started for the study. Each step felt heavy, as if

someone had put lead weights in her shoes. This was nonsense! She knew her own mind. She straightened her shoulders and rapped at the door.

"Come," her father said.

Julia eased into the room. Her father was seated behind his desk, papers strewn about before him. On seeing her, his frown eased, and he leaned back in his chair.

"There's my girl. What can I do for you? Velvet for a new gown? Bonnet need trimming?"

"Nothing so mundane, Father," Julia assured him, moving into the room. "I wanted to tell you that I can argue with you no longer. Lord Westerbrook is not the man for me."

He tossed his pencil down on his papers. "Thank the good Lord! I always said you were a clever chit."

She grimaced. "Yes, well, this took a bit longer than I'd like to reach a decision. But at least I now know exactly what I want in a husband—someone who encourages me, stands beside me, and pays me the honor, love, and respect I'm due. Someone who shares my vision for the future."

His smile faded with each word. "Lofty goals. Why do I think you'll tell me you've already found this paragon?"

Her hands knit before her gown. "I may have. I'm falling in love with Tanner."

"I was afraid of that," he said with a sigh. "It's only natural you would develop feelings after he saved your life during that robbery. But you need to know something about your Tanner. He has other plans for his future than to play bodyguard to an heiress. I had to pay the fellow a pretty penny to pretend an engagement with you."

Tanner fell away from the paneling, heart pounding as if he'd just battled a dozen French soldiers. He'd been shocked when Mrs. Daring had pulled out the books and shown him the way to listen in on his employer's conversation. It was dishonorable, unthinkable.

"Do you want to listen or shall I?" she'd asked when he'd hesitated.

"I will listen," he'd said. "This once."

Now he wished he hadn't. As he stepped further away from the wall, he heard the door of the study slam, then Julia's heels clacking down the corridor, fast.

Angry.

He caught his fists coming up in defense and forced them down.

She burst into the room, chest heaving and eyes flashing. "You lied to me."

"Oh, dear," Mrs. Daring said, scuttling toward the door. "I believe I left my embroidery upstairs."

She darted around Julia and disappeared.

"I thought we had an agreement," Julia said, stalking closer.

He backed up and bumped against the open bookshelf. She took in the tumble of books around him, the door hanging open behind, then shook her head.

"I should chide you for listening to my father's conversation, but I've done it a time or two myself. But I never led you to believe something that wasn't true."

Tanner held up his hands, palm out. "Your father is my employer. I owe him a duty."

"*I* am the one you are guarding," she threw back at him. "You owe me the truth."

"You asked me to lie to your father," he pointed out. "Pretend we were engaged."

She crossed her arms over her chest. "The entire point was to force him to see Lord Westerbrook in a new light. He could hardly do so if he was supreme in the knowledge that the viscount had no real competition."

His throat was tightening. "Then you have decided to stay the course and marry Westerbrook." He lowered his hands, defeat washing over him.

"Actually," she said, "I've decided Lord Westerbrook is a ninny with more concern for his consequence than anything or anyone else. I thought I was falling in love with you. My mistake."

The words cut into him. "Julia," he said, taking a step toward her.

She held up one hand. "Stop. You may not use my first name. That is reserved for friends and family. You are neither. You will obviously do anything to please your employer and advance your career, regardless of the consequences or the promises made to others. I do not want you as my bodyguard. You are discharged of duty."

He had never begged for anything in his life, but he begged now. "Julia, Miss Hewett, please. I never meant to hurt you. I'm falling in love with you too."

Tears were gathering in her dark eyes. "You, sir, have no concept of love. Pack your things and leave. At once."

She turned on her heel and marched out the door.

Leaving his hopes, his future, his very honor in tatters at his feet.

CHAPTER SEVENTEEN

JULIA'S RIGHTEOUS INDIGNATION carried her only until dinner. Daring had made herself scarce, and Julia hardly wanted to speak to her father, so she spent much of the afternoon stalking about the house, straightening paintings on the wall, centering vases on credenzas, tugging bed hangings into place. How could he have lied to her? She'd believed in him, trusted him, begun to think of him as a permanent part of her life. How had she so mistaken him?

"And Fortune approved of him!" she scolded the bust of some Roman fellow her father had installed on one of the landings.

The former Caesar regarded her with a surprisingly judgmental look.

When it was time for dinner, she stomped into the room, head high and spirit justified. But one look across the table, where no place had been set for Tanner, and all her anger fizzled away, leaving her empty.

"What's this, then, Garrison?" her father demanded of their butler, who was directing the footmen to serve. "Where's Tanner's plate? For that matter, where's Tanner?"

"It is my understanding that Mr. Tanner is no longer employed by this household, sir," Garrison said, calmly pouring her father's drink.

Her father leaned back to eye him. "Well, I certainly never sacked him. Who told you that rot?"

Garrison glanced to Daring, who looked to Julia.

She sat straighter. "I discharged Tanner, Father. I no longer had need of his services."

Her father frowned as Garrison moved out of range with surprising speed.

"I thought you two were engaged," her father grumbled.

Julia sliced into her pork roast. "You thought nothing of the kind. You asked him to pretend an engagement."

"Ah." Her father addressed his own loaded plate. "Told you, did he? Well, I warned him what would happen if he went against my wishes."

Julia scowled at him. "You asked him to lie?"

"So did you, my girl. Tit for tat."

Guilt rolled up like a carriage and parked on her chest. "I suppose you're right. I didn't like the way you tried to arrange my life, so I concocted a plan to stop it."

"Conversation can be so trying," Daring murmured. "Small wonder so few truly attempt it."

Julia swallowed. "Forgive me, Father. I shouldn't have asked Tanner to lie to you. I should have simply stood my ground and told you that I will be the one to decide who I marry. In my defense, I did try to tell you that, on multiple occasions. You didn't seem disposed to listen."

Her father nodded slowly. "I generally take the advice I need and ignore anyone who suggests I might try something else. I'm sorry I put you in that camp. Your message has been received. I'll stop pushing fellows on you. Though, mind you, it would please me no end if you could see your way to falling in love with a duke."

The piece of roast was still on her fork, uneaten. "I doubt that will happen," she said, trying to convince herself to take a bite, "but I'll keep it in mind." She set down the fork and met her father's gaze. "Honestly, Father, I don't think I have another Season in me. It's all been so disappointing."

"Here now," her father protested, brow puckering.

"This isn't like you. Where's my fiery daughter, ready to take on the world?"

"She seems to have gone up in her own flames," Julia said with a sigh.

"From the ashes rises the phoenix," Daring murmured.

Her father frowned at her companion as if he had no idea what she was talking about, but Julia understood. Perhaps she too, like the bird of legend, could find a way to start over from the disaster she'd made. Perhaps she had indulged her impetuous nature once too often.

She looked to their butler, who was now standing by the wall. "Has Mr. Tanner truly gone, Garrison?"

"Packed his weapons and left this afternoon, miss." He did not sound overly saddened by the fact.

Her father nodded. "He'll have returned to Rose Hill. I'll call on Lady Belfort tomorrow and see what can be done."

She should likely go as well. At the very least, she owed him an apology. But the thought of admitting her failings before an even greater audience than the man she'd thought she loved shriveled her stomach. Perhaps it would be enough to grovel when her father convinced him to come back to Hewett House.

"Thank you, Father," she said. "Please let him know that I will not give him any further trouble."

Her father cocked a smile. "Oh, I wouldn't promise that, my girl. Trouble has been your middle name since the day you were born."

"Father!" she protested, but his chuckle brought out a smile at last, and she was able to finish her dinner.

"The wind seems to have changed direction," Daring said as they adjourned to the library. Julia caught herself gazing at the bookcase where Tanner had usually stood and forced herself to look at her companion instead. Daring was watching her, head cocked.

"I hadn't noticed the weather," Julia said, taking the

chair opposite her and holding her hands toward the glowing fire. "Though I will admit to feeling a chill in the air."

"And your feelings toward Mr. Tanner, perhaps?"

She swallowed the lump in her throat. "It would be unwise to have feelings for Mr. Tanner."

Daring frowned. "Why? You just stood your ground to your father, and he seems to have agreed to follow your lead. I took that to mean you could choose who you liked."

Julia dropped her gaze to her fingers in her lap. "I said some rather harsh things to him after you left, Daring. I wouldn't blame him for doubting I could love him."

Daring tutted. "For a young lady who is adept at filling silence to the brim, you do on occasion forget to employ your words."

Julia threw up her hands. "Oh, so now I don't talk enough?"

"About important things, dear. How you feel, what you want. I'm not sure when you stopped trusting those around you to listen. But I encourage you to keep trying."

She nodded. "I will. If Father can bring him back to us, I'll apologize first thing."

"And?" Daring pressed, brows up.

Julia drew in a breath. "And tell him I still admire him above all other men."

Daring patted her hand. "Very wise. Just remember, actions can speak as loud as words."

"Why, Daring," Julia said, stifling a giggle, "are you telling me to kiss him?"

Daring raised her chin and withdrew her hand. "I'm sure I never said anything of the sort. What kind of companion do you take me for?"

Julia couldn't help laughing at that.

By morning, however, she was once more doubting

herself. All her life, she'd acted on any whim that pleased her. Could she dampen that tendency for anyone?

Even for Tanner?

She wrapped a shawl around her shoulders and stood in the doorway, watching as the carriage took her father off to Rose Hill. Instead of Tanner, her hopes sat on the bench with the coachman. She shivered.

"All will be well," Daring predicted as Julia returned to the house and Garrison shut the door. "Why don't we continue our plans for the clothing collection?"

"Of course," Julia said, and they ambled together down the corridor for the library.

But she found it no easier to attend to the pieces of paper and Daring's suggestions than she had the previous day. Would her father be persuasive? Would Tanner forgive her? Would he take her in his arms and press his lips to hers as a pledge for their future?

"And perhaps the Duke of Wey could be persuaded to donate his first-born son," Daring said.

Julia blinked. "Lord Thalston is a perfectly lovely lad. Why would his father donate him and to what purpose?"

"Oh, good," Daring said. "You've returned to us."

Julia shook her head. "Sorry. I'm just worried about seeing Tanner again. This temper of mine will be the death of me."

"Nonsense," Daring said, straightening her notes. "You are clever, Julia, and you have a good heart. You are fully capable of reining in your temper. As the only daughter of a doting father, such behavior was never expected of you, so naturally you lack practice."

Julia chuckled. "Much more practice, and I'll likely alienate everyone I know!"

"Your true friends will stand by you," Daring predicted.

As if in response to her words, the knocker sounded. Julia had popped to her feet, heart pounding, before realizing neither her father nor Tanner would need to knock.

She heard the door open and the footman on duty murmur what was most likely a welcome.

"Is Miss Hewett at home?" Elspeth's voice was high and sharp. "Please tell her I must speak to her."

With a glance at Daring, Julia headed for the door, her companion at her heels.

Elspeth saw her before the footman did and pushed past him to meet her. She'd forgotten a bonnet, and her round face was ashen. "Oh! Julia, please, you must help me!"

Julia took her hands and gave them a squeeze. "Of course! What's happened?"

"Father insists that I marry the Marquess of Norfall. He's nearly three times my age!"

"And has the most appalling taste in literature," Daring offered.

"Miss Bee and I will be in the upstairs withdrawing room," Julia told the footman, who was hovering uncertainly. "Will you have tea sent up?"

"Right away, miss," he promised, shutting the front door.

Julia led Elspeth up the stairs, Daring following. She made sure her friend was situated on the sofa near the hearth before dropping down beside her. "Now, then, what's this about forcing a marriage?"

Elspeth nodded so fast her curls bounced beside her face. "Mother told me this morning. I'm to marry him by special license next week. Oh, Julia, I simply can't!"

Julia's temper was building a head of steam, like the boiler in her father's engine. Such injustice! Was Elspeth to have no say in her life?

And was this not a chance to practice control?

Julia raised her chin. "I was not impressed with the

marquess when he called here, but perhaps he has good qualities."

Elspeth stared at her. "I thought you'd be on my side!"

Julia clasped one of her hands anew. "I am, I promise you. I was just trying to consider the possible advantages."

"I know the so-called advantages," Elspeth said, sniffing back tears. "He's wealthy. He has a title. He'll likely die and leave me all his money."

"Goodness, did your mother say that?" Julia asked, shocked.

"She isn't wrong, dear," Daring put in.

"She isn't right either," Elspeth countered. "And yes, she did tell me that. Along with some nonsense about closing my eyes and doing my duty for England. I don't want to spend my marriage doing my duty for England!"

"Certainly not," Julia agreed. Her temper was rolling down the track, ready to crush anything in its way. She slammed on the brakes. "There must be an alternative."

Elspeth nodded. "There is. I've already given my heart to Adrian Keller."

She'd thought as much. "Did you tell your mother?"

"No," Elspeth admitted, hanging her head. "You know my mother, Julia. Once she has her mind made up, nothing will dissuade her."

"I've recently been reminded that we must be honest with those we love," Julia said, glancing to Daring, who nodded encouragement. "Your mother may have strong opinions, on any number of topics, but it is clear that she loves you, Elspeth. She always speaks of you in the most glowing terms to any who will listen."

"And to those who listen under duress," Daring agreed.

"I know she loves me," Elspeth said as the footman carried in the tea tray. "And she wants me to be happy. She's simply convinced I'll be happier as a marchioness than the wife of an Imperial Guard."

"A former Imperial Guard," Julia said. "Has he found no position yet?"

She sighed. "None. Oh, but these employers are blind! How could they not make an offer to the kindest, most thoughtful, gentlest man in England?"

Precisely because the work Mr. Keller might be asked to perform required none of those traits, but Julia decided not to mention that. There was honesty, and there was cruelty.

"Nevertheless, you must tell your mother and father how you feel," she urged Elspeth. "A dear friend helped me see that we must stand our ground on matters such as these. I have perhaps trampled the ground and shouted my way through, which I do not advise. Calm determination will win the day."

"Do you really think so?" Elspeth asked.

"I hope so," Julia said as Daring began pouring the tea. "But I also take solace in the fact that they cannot force you to say the vows. No clergyman will marry you without that."

Elspeth nodded. "There is that." She accepted a cup from Daring and glanced around. "Where is your Mr. Tanner?"

"Out," Julia said.

Daring frowned at her.

She sighed. "Sorry, that is to say I lost my temper yesterday and threw him out. Father's at Rose Hill now attempting to patch things over. As soon as he returns with Tanner, I intend to apologize. Profusely. So, you see, I know from experience that calm is better than erupting in emotion."

"However satisfying," Elspeth agreed, lifting her cup.

From the front of the house, voices shouted. Quinn and Pulvey thundered down the corridor. Julia and Elspeth exchanged glances even as Daring set aside her cup and stood.

Candy appeared in the doorway, face as white as the cap on her dark hair. "Begging your pardon, Miss Hewett, but your father's been attacked by those highwaymen. Mr. Garrison is sending for the physician."

Julia rose on shaky legs. "Elspeth, I…"

"Go," Elspeth said, setting aside her cup and rising as well. "I'll see if there's anything I can do to help."

Tanner sheltered under an oak at the western edge of the Hewett estate. The long, dark fingers of the branches, mostly bare now, reached in every direction, as if trying to grasp the house beyond and pull it closer. He knew the feeling. He'd wanted to take Julia in his arms, apologize for the lie that had parted them, promise he'd honor her above all others in the future.

He'd spent a cold, damp night nestled under leathery, evergreen shrubs across the road, trying to determine his next move. He could go back to Rose Hill, admit to Lady Belfort that he'd failed in the charge she'd given him. It was only her due. Trust between bodyguard and guarded was imperative, and he had broken it. Worse, he'd developed feelings for the woman he was supposed to be guarding.

But his love for Julia was the very reason he couldn't just quit the area. He'd camped under far worse conditions during the war, with little more than what he had now. Rain and hard ground were no strangers. Nothing was more important than Julia's wellbeing. Until he knew the threats to her had been resolved, how could he move on?

At least her father's insistence on a view in every direction meant it was easy to keep an eye on the house. He'd seen the carriage leave and disappear along the Weybridge Road in the direction of Weyton. Then he'd spotted the Bee carriage arriving. Of more concern was the precipitous return of the Hewett coach. The footmen had carried someone into the house, but Julia was obviously entertaining Elspeth Bee, so he knew it wasn't her. Had something happened to her father?

He'd relocated to the oak for a better view but had only seen a small carriage arrive. A physician, perhaps?

He pulled his gaze from the house and swept the area. The kitchen garden, where he'd first caught the scent of Julia's perfume, lay empty. So did the lawn where she'd taken his hand and the field where they'd kissed.

Was everything in his life now to be judged by its connection to her?

He forced his gaze to keep moving. Pepin was exercising a horse in the paddock next to the stables. He must have been demoted back to his previous position with Tanner sent away. Perhaps he could mention the lad to Lady Belfort. Pepin deserved the opportunity to advance.

He had come full circle on his scan of the area. Even the road to Weybridge stood empty, with no wagon, carriage, or horse and rider in sight. The only movement came from the hedgerow across from the house. It was trembling.

Odd. He glanced up at the oak, but its gnarled branches lay still. Yet the bushes swayed, as if pulled by unseen hands. The movement was too large for the small animals that usually frequented the hedgerow. Could a cow have become entangled on the other side?

Or was there more afoot?

Tanner dropped to the ground and crept through the tall grass until he was right next to the road. The rumble to the west told him a wagon was coming at last. He waited until it passed him to dart across the road in the dust and squeeze through a gap in the brush. Moving from tree to tree and bush to bush, he crept closer to where he had seen the bushes moving, the scent of decaying branches nearly as sharp as the thorns that caught at his coat.

And then he spotted them: three men, hunkered down

like he was and watching the house. He flattened himself to the ground and eased closer with his elbows.

"Did you have to hit him so hard?" he heard one complain, his rough coat looking as if it had come from a much larger fellow. "We were only supposed to scare him."

One of his companions snorted. "That sort doesn't scare easily. At least he knows we're serious."

"Either way, we've earned our fee," the third put in in a deep bass. "Just one more job, lads, and we'll be set for life."

The first climbed to his feet, and recognition hit. It was the taller man from the robbery. But Tanner had only identified his companion as the shorter robber when his words hit harder.

"If you ask me, we'd be smarter to keep the heiress and ransom her ourselves. I bet she's worth a pretty penny."

CHAPTER EIGHTEEN

TANNER'S BLOOD RAN cold. He had drawn himself into a crouch and pulled one of his throwing knives from his boot before he'd thought better of it, but he stayed his hand. There were three of them, and as the other two stood as well, he could see pistols in belts and knives at their hips. He and Roth had subdued two. If Tanner couldn't defeat them all, who would save Julia?

He slid the knife back into place and waited, listening. It was one of the hardest things he'd ever done.

The tallest of the three cuffed his comrade on the shoulder. "We ransom her ourselves, we risk getting caught. We do it the way his lordship suggested, and he'll see we get off, scot-free, just as he did at the robbery. I'd rather have a good price with no risk than take a chance at a greater price where I might lose my neck."

His lordship? Could they mean Westerbrook? Why would he want Julia kidnapped? And why help these men escape justice?

His friend shrugged. "Oh, all right. Have it your way. He's been right so far. Even putting those notes in the mail didn't get us in trouble."

"So, we'll stay with the plan," the other said. "His lordship said he would be coming to call tomorrow. We'll take the heiress then."

Not if Tanner had anything to say about the matter.

Julia paced the corridor outside her father's bedchamber.

"Doctor Shoring is very good, I've found," Daring offered. Her companion had requested that the footmen bring two chairs on which she and Julia could sit while they waited. Only Daring had actually sat.

"He'd be better if he'd allow me into the room while he examines Father," Julia complained as she passed.

"Men prefer their privacy in such matters," Daring said. "Women too."

Fortunately, the door opened just then, and the physician came out. He removed his spectacles and aimed his deep-set grey eyes at Julia.

"You may go in, Miss Hewett," he said with a lift of his bushy brown brows. "But he likely won't be conscious once he takes the laudanum I've prescribed."

He stepped aside to allow her past.

Her father was lying in the center of his large bed, pillows behind him and covers pulled up. His hair showed in a tuft of red above the white bandage wrapping his head. But his blue eyes were crackling as she approached.

Julia perched on the chair beside the bed. "How are you feeling?"

"Like a fool," he grumbled, mustache tipping up on one side. "I should have given those rogues what for."

She tucked in the covers nearest her. "I can't help thinking this is my fault."

"Don't be daft," he snapped. "You hardly told the highwaymen where to find me."

"I might as well have," she said with a sniff. "I'm the one who sent our bodyguard off with his tail between his legs."

"*Your* bodyguard," her father corrected her. "I can take care of myself. Or so I thought." He shifted against the pillows.

Julia reached for the little brown bottle on the bedside table. "Do you need something for the pain?"

Her father waved her away with one hand. "Never have before. Besides, that stuff used to put your mother fast asleep when she was ailing."

Julia lowered the bottle to the table with trembling fingers. "I remember. Oh, Father, are you sure you'll be all right? I don't want to lose you too!"

His face softened. "There now, my girl. You can't keep an old dog like me down. I'll be up in time for dinner."

"Well, we'll see," Julia said, setting her hands back in her lap. "I only wish you'd had Tanner with you. He wouldn't come back from Rose Hill?"

"He wasn't at Rose Hill," her father said. "Lady Belfort hadn't seen him, and neither had his pals. I even checked the inn in the village. Nothing."

Julia's stomach plummeted. "Then where could he be? You don't think the highwaymen…"

"They'd be even more daft to take on someone of his skills," her father insisted. "No, he's gone into hiding, though I don't know why. His friends will be looking for him." He grimaced and shifted on the pillows again.

"You should have given in to them," Julia scolded. "We can make do with the loss of some silver or jewelry. We can't make do without you."

Her father frowned. "Funny, that. They never demanded money or my watch. They insisted I climb out of the coach and then lay into me."

Julia shuddered. "I'm just glad you're alive."

"Me too," her father promised her. "Now, would you go see what that physician told Cook about what I can eat? I could do with a good bit of roast or ham tonight, not some miserly gruel."

"I'll see what I can do." She rose, pressed a kiss against his cheek, and left him.

Daring was waiting in the corridor. "The physician has gone. How is your father?"

"As testy as always," Julia told her. "But he relayed some surprising news. Tanner isn't at Rose Hill or the inn."

Daring tsked, falling into step beside her as Julia headed toward the stairs. "Someone else hired him. I knew it."

"No, that's just it." Julia stopped on the landing. "No one knows where he is. He's disappeared." This time, her breath caught. "Oh, Daring, I'm so worried. What if something happens to him because I couldn't keep my temper?"

"He's a smart fellow," Daring said, turning for the stairs. "I'm sure he'll be fine. I believe you mentioned giving me a half day off. Would now be convenient?"

Julia stared as her diminutive companion descended the stairs. "Now?" she asked, scurrying to follow. "With Father hurt and Tanner missing?"

Daring reached the bottom and glanced back at her. "Well, I really can't do much about either, dear. And you do seem to need time to think."

Perhaps she did. And she knew she'd been imposing on her companion. "Very well. Will you have dinner with us?"

"I certainly hope so, but don't wait for me." And she disappeared down the corridor for the servant's stair.

Tanner had never excelled at tracking. That was more Roth's specialty, though they had all learned the skill to some extent while in the army. French and British soldiers had the luxury of marching across open fields to fight each other. Batavaria had few flat fields. Her troops knew better how to fight on the rocky mountain slopes, using the terrain as protection. So, after waiting for the highwaymen to move on, he kept one knife in hand and moved from tree to tree, watchful for any movement ahead as he attempted to follow them to their camp.

Instead, a noise behind him had him whirling, knife up and at the ready.

A tiny figure was strutting toward him. Swathed in a heavy wool cloak, black velvet bonnet on her head, she used a walking stick to swat away branches and shrubs as if they were encroaching suitors.

Had he gone mad? "Mrs. Daring?"

"Ah, I thought I might find you nearby," she said with a pleasant smile, as if they were meeting in the library at Hewett House.

He glanced around her. "Is Julia, that is Miss Hewett, with you?"

"No, dear. I thought it better if we had this conversation bodyguard to bodyguard, as it were."

Tanner's gaze came back to her. Those blue eyes were sharper than ever as she stopped in front of him. By the lay of her cloak, she'd put one foot forward, one foot back, a stance a pugilist might take before raising his fists, and her walking stick was firmly planted.

"You're Julia's bodyguard," he realized.

"I have been since her dear mother hired me, yes." Even her breathless voice belied the statement. "I am skilled with pistol, knife, and staff, thanks to my dear husband, who protected the Royal Princes at one point in his illustrious career. Julia hasn't been nearly as much trouble, though I must say it's been delightful having someone else to help. I haven't had a day off in nearly a decade."

"Does Julia know?" Tanner asked, still trying to align what he saw with what he'd just been told.

"Neither Julia nor her father knows," she said. "Hence his desire to hire you."

Tanner shook his head. "You astound me. And I thought *my* position untenable."

"It has not been without some challenges," she acknowledged. "You, unfortunately, are the latest." She shook a finger at him. "You shouldn't have run off like that. Everyone is worried."

"I didn't run off. I spent the night keeping watch."

"And left Mr. Hewett to go haring off this morning to bring you back from Rose Hill only to be accosted by those terrible highwaymen as a result."

He rocked back on his heels. "So, that's who they brought into the house." And who the highwaymen had been describing. "Is he all right?"

"Injured," she said. "But expected to recover. Julia, however, is another case entirely."

He couldn't breathe, yet words poured out. "Is she hurt? How badly? Why didn't you say that first!"

She held up her free hand, palm toward him, as if he were a spooked horse. "Easy. She is unharmed physically, but I do believe her heart is broken. She is quite in love with you."

Hope shoved past his fear, allowing breath to come easier. "And I love her. But her father will never agree to us marrying."

"Perhaps," she said with maddening calm. "And perhaps he might. In the meantime, I do hope you'll return to the house. It feels frightfully cold out here. My bones aren't what they used to be."

He found he couldn't believe that. Someone who had faithfully safeguarded Julia for more than ten years was made of the stuff of legend. And he would always be grateful to her. But there was more she should know.

"The cold isn't the issue." He went on to tell her about the highwaymen, their plans, and his suspicions about Lord Westerbrook. When he finished, her face was grim.

"What do you intend to do?" she asked, fingering her staff. "Three well-armed men might be a bit much even for you."

Tanner couldn't help his smile. "Ready to join me, are you?"

"If I must."

He shook his head in admiration. "Rest assured, I won't let them escape this time. As soon as I find their camp, I'll alert Rose Hill and the duke. There will be far more than two of us taking them on."

"Very wise," she said. "In the meantime, I'll remain watchful. Together, we'll keep her safe."

Together. Funny. He had never become accustomed to sharing duties with the other guards, preferring the work that required him to act alone. Now, he had to rely on a little, elderly woman to keep the lady he loved safe.

Somehow, he didn't think Julia could be in better hands.

In the end, Tanner followed the highwaymen as far as their camp, which was closer to Weyton, then requested a ride from a farmer on the Weybridge Road into the village and on to Rose Hill. He could see why the duke and his agents were having trouble finding the criminals. The camp lay in a hollow surrounded by hawthorns, with a single, narrow entrance nearly eclipsed by a clump of lilacs. So long as they only lit a fire after dark, no one would be the wiser.

As the grey autumn afternoon darkened toward evening, Tanner, Keller, Roth, and three men the duke had enlisted positioned themselves at the mouth of the draw. The cold air sat heavily in Tanner's chest as he waited for Roth's signal to move forward. The older guardsman had been given leave by his employer to assist in the capture, and the three local men had seemed relieved to put him in charge of the group. Tanner was glad as well. Mrs. Daring was right—he could do only so much on his own. He needed the help of others.

Especially Julia.

It was becoming more and more difficult to imagine a future without her. But even if she forgave him, would she be willing to settle for an adventurer when she might have had a duke?

Keller and one of the other men had squeezed down the narrow entrance when Roth beckoned to Tanner. With a nod, he slipped past the lilacs. Though the flowers had been reduced to dry brown husks that rattled in the breeze, he fancied he still caught their scent.

For Julia.

Roth slid in behind him and tapped him on the shoulder. Tanner tapped the man in front of him. A moment more, and Keller's cry went up.

"In the name of the king, drop your weapons and stand down. You are under arrest!"

Before the last word echoed, all six of them had burst into the clearing and surrounded the highwaymen, who had been seated around a circle of blackened stones.

The shortest raised his hands.

"We've done nothing wrong," the taller whined, one hand still on the knife he'd been using to skin some small creature.

"Drop it," Roth ordered, pistol in one hand.

The knife hit the ground with a puff of dust.

The third rose. In the growing twilight, his face looked lined and haggard. "We're just moving through. You've no call to trouble us."

Tanner had had enough. "We know you're the highwaymen who have been preying on travelers in the area. We know you attacked John Hewett and intend to kidnap his daughter."

They exchanged glances.

The man on his feet curled his lip. "You don't know any of that. You're guessing."

"I don't have to guess," Tanner said. "I had it from Lord Westerbrook."

Roth and Keller stared at him.

The taller surged to his feet. "I knew it! I knew we couldn't trust him!"

"Shut up!" the other warned.

The short fellow sagged. "Why? He's given us up. We'll never get the money he promised."

"Enough!" Roth barked. "Tie their hands and take them out to the wagon. The duke has a dark corner of his dungeon waiting for them."

As the other men went to work, Keller sidled closer to Tanner. "I thought Castle Wey lacked a dungeon," he murmured, keeping his pistol trained on the highwaymen.

"They don't need to know that," Tanner murmured back.

Keller's smile quickly faded. "And Westerbrook? He should be punished as well, but I have heard that England has different rules for a lord than a commoner."

He had heard the same. "You, I, and Roth can deal with Westerbrook."

Keller frowned. "How?"

"His lordship is expecting to be attacked by highwaymen tomorrow," Tanner said. "It would be a shame to disappoint him."

Daring had suggested that Julia needed time to think. While she agreed in theory, the act proved entirely impractical. She sat in her suite, but she kept listening for any sounds farther down the corridor from her father's room. No one came to fetch her, so she could only conclude he was resting. She'd already reported that Cook was planning baked sturgeon with mushrooms for dinner, and her father had been willing to content himself with that.

She moved to the library instead, but she found herself staring at the spot where Tanner had stood again, remembering his quick smiles, his stories about his father. She pushed off from the sofa and stalked to the upstairs withdrawing room, but the view across the fields just reminded her of their last ride together.

Their kiss.

An aberration, she'd called it then, thinking her mind made up about Lord Westerbrook. She should have realized her mind was indeed made up, only it, along with her heart, had decided on Tanner instead.

Why was she sitting and thinking? Better to try and find him. Yes, he was perfectly capable of taking care of himself, but everyone needed help once in a while, even her father. She started for the door, about to call for her cloak and bonnet, only to slow to a stop on the carpet.

It wasn't just her temper she needed to fight. It was this impetuous nature of hers. For once in her life, she really should plan. She had no idea where to even begin looking. And it wasn't wise to go riding about alone with highwaymen on the loose.

She paced the room a moment, then strode out into the entry hall. Garrison, who had apparently been instructing Pulvey on some task, stopped and offered her a smile.

"Miss Hewett, how might I be of service?"

"Daring and I will dine with my father in his room tonight. If you'd let the staff know."

"Of course."

"And if I may borrow Mr. Pulvey, I will check the outbuildings of the estate, in case Mr. Tanner thought to make use of them."

Garrison's cheek was so taut she might have bounced a ball off it. "Mr. Pulvey and Mr. Quinn are, alas, busy."

Pulvey frowned, then quickly ducked his head.

"Then I'll go alone," Julia announced. "Wandering off, into the wilderness, beyond the reach of help. If you'd be so kind as to fetch my pelisse, bonnet, and gloves?"

He opened his mouth to argue, she was sure, but he

seemed to think better of it, for he turned to the footman. "Fetch Miss Hewett's belongings, Pulvey, and escort her wherever she wants to go."

Pulvey went running.

It was only logical, she thought as she walked down to the stables a short time later, her footman a few respectful feet behind. If she had gone missing, surely Tanner would have searched the estate buildings first. She started with the stables, but none there had seen him. Young Pepin looked particularly saddened by the fact. It was the same in the little stone buttery and the wash house. And both the garden sheds proved empty as well.

At least Daring returned in time to dine with Julia and her father. Her cheeks were pink, as if she'd gone for a walk in the cold too. She lay a hand on Julia's shoulder as they retired to her suite.

"Tomorrow will be much better, dear," she promised.

Julia could only hope so.

CHAPTER NINETEEN

JULIA WAS IN the library the next morning, attempting to convince Daring they should venture out and widen the search for Tanner, when Garrison showed in Lord Westerbrook. Once she would have been delighted to receive him. Now her first thought was, *oh bother!*

"Julia, dear," he said, holding out his hands as if he would take hers. Julia pretended not to notice and busied her fingers with smoothing her skirts.

"Lord Westerbrook," she said. "How kind of you to call. I'm afraid I wasn't expecting visitors today. My father has been injured."

His mouth dipped down at the corners. "So I heard. It was the talk of Weyton when we drove through. My poor darling. How are you bearing up?"

Odd that he would stop to ask people he had never met about the local gossip, but perhaps he had heard it at his cousin's if he had stayed the night there.

"I'm fine," she said. "And so is Father. Thank you for coming."

"Of course. But you must let me take your mind off your troubles. Come driving with me."

Daring glanced out the window, where a leaden sky promised rain or even snow. "I wouldn't advise it. It's much too cold."

"I have heated bricks and blankets in the coach," he told them both. "Besides, our company will keep us warm."

Had she ever been attracted to such pap? She could only bless Daring for interceding on her behalf again.

"As Miss Hewett's companion and chaperone," she said, "I cannot allow her to travel in a closed carriage even with a gentleman of your impeccable reputation, my lord. I'm sure you understand."

His smile looked the slightest bit strained. "Of course. We'd be delighted to have you join us, madam."

Would he persist? She had in mind to give him a stern rejoinder when a better idea popped up.

"Would you be willing to follow the Weybridge Road toward Weyton, my lord?" She could look for Tanner while they drove!

"Wherever you like," he said with an expansive wave.

Daring sneezed. "Oh, dear. Julia, we really cannot expose ourselves to a confined space with his lordship. Remember his malady?"

"Entirely recovered, dear lady," he insisted. "Please say you'll come."

Julia cast Daring a quelling glance. "I'll have Garrison bring our coats."

In short order, she and Daring were installed in Lord Westerbrook's carriage, Julia and her companion on one side, his lordship across from them. His bricks had long since gone cold, but the wool blankets went a long way toward keeping her warm.

As he chattered on about doings in London, she kept her gaze trained out the window, looking for any sign that Tanner might have been that way. Were Imperial Guards skilled at woodcraft? She saw no indication of anyone camping—no smoke rising, no obvious break in the bushes.

"I know this may not be the right time or place," Lord Westerbrook said, "but I hope you know that I hold you in the highest esteem, Julia."

The last phrase warned her what was coming, and she turned her gaze to his. "Thank you. But…"

He held up one hand. "Please, hear me out. We gentlemen take some trouble in composing our proposals."

Oh, no. He was going to propose. After all this time!

"I understand," she said with a gentle smile. "Perhaps I can make the whole affair easier on you."

"Oh, darling, you've made me so happy!" he said, beaming. "I've already applied at Doctor's Commons for a special license. We can be married tomorrow, if you wish."

Julia shook her head. "No, my lord, that's not what I meant."

"Why is the coach slowing?" Daring put in.

Lord Westerbrook joined Julia in peering out the window. They were near the edge of her father's estate, where the woods stretched toward the next field. She heard a call, a voice that she had been longing to hear since the moment she had sacked him.

"Stop this coach!"

Lord Westerbrook raised his head as the coach stopped. "We are being attacked, but never fear, Julia, dear. I promise no harm will come to you."

"No, my lord," Julia started, but Daring put a hand on her arm. Julia glanced her way. Her companion shook her head, face surprisingly stern.

Lord Westerbrook unlatched the door and pushed it open, then stepped down.

"Gentlemen," he said, hands up, "there's no need for this. We will turn over whatever you want."

"We want the heiress," someone said, voice sounding muffled.

No! She would not believe Tanner in league with highwaymen. Or was she going mad to think she'd heard his voice?

"Do exactly as I tell you," Daring said beside her in a tone Julia had never heard before.

"Surely you would not expect me to turn over my dearest love," Lord Westerbrook was saying. "I have a gold pocket watch and a pouch of silver. Take those instead."

A sharper voice interrupted. "We'll take the watch, the silver, and the heiress. Be quick about it."

Wait, was that Mr. Roth?

She broke away from Daring and chanced a peek out the carriage window. Three men stood near the horses, masks up over their noses and mouths and hats pulled down to shadow their eyes, but she thought she caught a glimpse of russet hair on the foremost fellow. And she knew that many-caped greatcoat.

"Very well," the man who had just proposed to her said. "You give me no choice but to yield to your superior forces. But you will rue the day you dared to trouble the fiancée of Lord Westerbrook."

She collapsed back in her seat and stared at Daring. "He's giving me up!"

"Well, he is a coward, dear," Daring said. "Perhaps we should indulge him, just to see what else he might offer. We both know those aren't really highwaymen." She reached around her and opened the door of the carriage. "After you."

Julia climbed down from the coach and raised her chin. Beyond Lord Westerbrook, Tanner stood, pistol in his grip, watching. The slightly taller man must be Mr. Roth, so that meant the one with the twinkling eyes must be Mr. Keller.

She marched past Lord Westerbrook. "I am severely disappointed in you, my lord. You claim that you wish to marry me, but the man I love would do anything to protect me. He would lie, spend the night in open fields, and even pretend to be a highwayman." Her gaze met Tanner's.

Tanner peeled the mask from his face. "You knew."

"I recognized your voice," she said. Then she gave in to her nature and threw herself into his arms. For a moment, she gloried in the strength around her.

"What is this?" Lord Westerbrook demanded behind her. "Who are you?"

"Those come to see you punished for your deeds," Mr. Roth intoned.

She turned to find that the other two guardsmen had now arranged themselves on either side of the viscount. He glanced from one to the other, then his gaze lit on Tanner.

"Why should I be punished?" He pointed at Tanner. "There is your villain. He obviously orchestrated all of this to prove his worth and force Hewett to keep him on staff. Why would you need a bodyguard if there's no danger?"

Tanner's jaw tightened. Julia offered him a smile. "You will never make me believe that, my lord. Kristof Tanner will always be a hero in my eyes."

His face relaxed. "So long as you are safe, Julia. That's all that matters."

"Not entirely." She looked once more on the man she had thought to marry. "You, my lord, are a sorry excuse for a human being. I never want to lay eyes on you again."

Red blotched his face. "After all I've done for you!"

Her brows rose. "Have you done *anything* for me?"

"He had your neighbors and your father assaulted," Daring said, ticking the facts off on her fingers. "He arranged for your kidnapping and maligned the man you love. I would say he's accomplished a great deal."

"You, madam, know nothing," he spat at her before turning once more to Julia, lips curling in a sneer. "I brought you to the notice of the right people. I allowed myself to pay you, a little country nobody, court. I proposed marriage! That should have been enough to have you at my feet, but you had to play coy."

Julia choked on her rising temper. "Coy! If you were half the man Tanner is, I would have fallen at your feet within minutes."

Tanner smothered a laugh.

Daring shook her head. "Never feed the weasels, dear. They tend to bite."

Indeed, Lord Westerbrook looked as if he wanted to snap her in two. But that wasn't why she drew in a breath through her nose and forced her shoulders down. It was another opportunity to practice, even if she thought her temper entirely justified this time.

"You, sir, are a worm," she contented herself with saying. "Never darken my door again."

"Oh, I'll be back," he threatened. "You may not have the breeding or the beauty I deserve, but your fortune is too good to forego. You will marry me. I'll see you and your family ruined if you don't."

Tanner released her to stalk up to the viscount. He seized the fellow by the scruff of the neck and shoved him to the door of the coach. As he had once before, he opened the door with his free hand and pushed Lord Westerbrook up the steps and into the carriage.

"You won't ruin anyone," Tanner told the viscount as Lord Westerbrook struggled to right himself and regain his dignity. "It would be the work of a minute to find a sample of your handwriting. I wager it will match the threatening notes Mr. Hewett received. We will be looking into your finances. A viscount who demands only an heiress must have something to hide."

Lord Westerbrook waxed white before Tanner shut the door and thumped on the side of the carriage. "Take him away."

The coachman touched his whip to his hat in salute and called to the horses. The carriage rolled off.

Julia applauded. "Oh, Tanner, that was famous."

He chuckled as Roth and Keller removed their masks to show the grins on their faces.

"You didn't approve the last time I sent him packing," Tanner reminded her.

"I didn't know I was in love with you last time," Julia said. "If I had, I would have been cheering you on then too."

He returned to her side, and the warmth of his gaze captured her more surely than any highwayman. As he bent his head, she raised her chin to meet him.

"You might want to hurry," Daring suggested. "Garrison seems to have noticed the so-called robbery. We'll shortly be surrounded."

Julia glanced toward the house. Mounted grooms were riding their way, and footmen were marching behind. She looked to Tanner.

He touched her cheek. "I have no right to love you, Julia. You were destined to marry a viscount, a duke, a prince."

"Instead, I will marry someone even finer," she said. "The man I love." She pressed her lips against his.

As his arms tightened around her, she slipped into the warmth. No one had ever made her feel this safe, this precious, this beautiful. This is what she had been seeking all those Seasons in London. This was the man she wanted to spend her life with. This was the man she loved.

She thought she heard Daring sigh. For once, it sounded happy.

CHAPTER TWENTY

"MORE TEA, SIR?" Garrison asked, hovering over Tanner with the silver pot as he sat with Julia beside her father's bed.

"Thank you, no, Garrison," Tanner said, mouth hinting of a smile.

"I could do with a bit more," Julia's father pointed out, lifting his cup over the bedcovers.

Garrison poured for him.

"I can see to the rest, Garrison," Julia told him, setting her own cup on the nearby side table.

"Of course, Miss Hewett, and may I say again how glad we all are that Mr. Tanner captured those scoundrels." His gaze to Tanner was almost worshipful.

"Yes, yes," her father said testily. "Tanner is the hero of the day. I'm just glad to know we've seen the last of those highwaymen and Lord Westerbrook."

"Perhaps a scone, Mr. Tanner?" Garrison asked, offering a plate.

"That will be all, Garrison," her father said. "Tell Cook I plan to eat at the table tonight."

"Very good, sir." Garrison bowed himself out.

"I see you've made a believer of that one," her father told Tanner before taking a sip of his tea.

"He inflates my contribution," Tanner said. "I would not have been effective alone. I see that now. My fellow guardsmen helped in the capture. And your staff is to be commended. They didn't know we'd changed places with the highwaymen. Pepin saw the coach stop and alerted the house. Mr. Garrison rallied the staff. And Mrs. Daring kept everyone calm. We owe them all much."

Julia could only agree.

"And I owe you an apology, Father," she said. "We have had entirely too many secrets in this house. I promise you to be honest with you in the future. And to that end, you should know that there is a weak spot on the wall between the study and the library that allows someone to listen to what you're saying there."

Tanner nodded to her in encouragement.

Her father stiffened. "What's this?"

"As far as I know, it's never been used for nefarious purposes," Julia promised him. "But I suggest you have it fixed."

He drew in a breath. "No, we'll leave it, so long as only family knows about it. If I ever behave badly again, you have my permission to use it."

"Thank you, Father." She glanced at Tanner, and he nodded again. She focused on her father. "Daring and Tanner also know, but I think we can agree that Daring is family, and Tanner is about to be." She reached out and took Tanner's hand. He squeezed her fingers.

Her father eyed their joined hands. "I see. And what have you to say for yourself, my lad?"

Tanner's gaze didn't leave hers. "I have no idea what I could have done to earn your daughter's love, sir, but I promise you I will always cherish it."

"Pretty words, but they won't fill an empty belly or keep coal in the hearth."

"Father," Julia scolded.

Her father held up one hand. "This is a discussion between me and your betrothed. Every groom has to prove himself to the lady's father first."

"Not before he proves himself to the lady," Julia

grumbled, but Tanner squeezed her hand again, and she nodded her trust to him.

"I may not be the duke you wanted, but I can provide for your daughter," Tanner told her father. "Julia and I would need to discuss the matter first, but I could apply for a post with Prince Otto Leopold. He will be returning to England as the first official ambassador for Württemberg. With her husband on his staff, Julia could remain close enough to visit you. My position would also give her entre to the highest circles of London Society."

Oh, the dear. It was exactly what her father had wanted for her, minus the ducal coronet and title. A shame it wasn't what she wanted. And she didn't think Tanner wanted it either. If he had intended to work for the prince, he would have gone with the delegation to Württemberg.

But her father nodded slowly. "That might suffice. Let's discuss income."

"That is entirely enough discussion, Father," Julia put in. "I am not something to be bartered. Besides, I have my own plans for the future." She turned to Tanner. "You know I have so dreamed of traveling. Would it disappoint you to leave your prince behind and come with me?"

Tanner brought her fingers to his lips and pressed a kiss against them, setting her to trembling. "Not a bit. I love you, Julia, and I would follow you to the ends of the earth."

Hope pulsed through her. "Good," she said. "Because I plan to take you to the ends of the earth, perhaps starting with those pyramids you described."

His gaze lit.

Her father slapped his hands down on the bedcovers. "That's settled, then."

Julia dropped Tanner's hand and stared at him. "That's it? You don't intend to argue the point, demand capitulation?"

"I've heard all about Tanner's feats of bravery from you,

Garrison, and young Pepin. The fellow put himself to some trouble to make sure you were safe and cared for. That's the sort of husband I want for my girl."

Julia leaned forward and kissed him on the cheek, then she kissed Tanner, not on the cheek. Somehow, no matter how far they traveled, no matter what they did, she thought she would always feel that thrill. Higher than a balloon, faster than a steam engine, straight to her heart.

Of course they had to go to Rose Hill the next day to tell everyone the good news. Julia, Tanner, and Daring arrived to find Elspeth already visiting, Fortune curled up in her lap. Julia's friend proudly showed her a simple gold engagement ring.

"I took your advice and told my mother and father exactly how I feel," she explained. "Father promptly offered Adrian a job working for him."

"Assistant to the head of the firm," Keller said with a wry grin as they all sat in Lady Belfort's withdrawing room, Fortune now making the rounds from person to person. "I am more than willing to learn, if it means Elspeth will be by my side."

She linked arms with him and beamed.

"I also have good news," Julia told them, smiling at Tanner. "Tanner and I will be married before Christmas. We plan to start for the Ottoman Empire in the new year."

Congratulations flowed all around.

Mr. Roth stood, drawing all eyes to him. He did not have Tanner's flair or Mr. Keller's boyish good looks, but there was a power and a presence about him in his simple navy coat and buff trousers.

"I am pleased my fellow guards have found such valiant, intelligent brides," he said. "They are honorable men, who will make exceptional husbands. Perhaps it will ease any concern to know that the highwaymen will be held for trial."

Elspeth looked to Mr. Keller as if for confirmation. Fortune raised her head as well.

Mr. Keller nodded. "They admitted to robbing several coaches over the summer, including Lord Westerbrook's when he was returning from visiting Lady Alldene. He made them a better offer. He would point out exactly who to rob and when."

Mr. Roth's dark eyes narrowed. "Are you telling this story, or am I?"

Mr. Keller waved a hand at him and sat back in his chair. Fortune dropped down and stalked up to Mr. Roth as if giving him her undivided attention.

Tanner winked at Julia, who hid a smile.

As Fortune sat in front of him, Mr. Roth expanded his already impressive chest. "Lord Westerbrook had given Rufus Jacobs money to invest in his canals. Before the man could deposit it, the highwaymen retrieved it for the viscount. His lordship was concerned Lord Norfall was pursuing Miss Hewett. The highwaymen eliminated his rival."

Tanner leaned forward. "They also implied that Westerbrook was the author of those anonymous notes, which they inserted into the post. I sent word to Lady Alldene this morning, hoping she can provide an example of his lordship's handwriting. He was trying to set the stage for Julia's kidnapping."

"So he could rescue me, prove himself to my father, and earn my undying devotion," Julia agreed. She looked to Tanner. "But my undying devotion was already given."

Tanner smiled. "And matched."

"And so the area is safe," Mr. Roth concluded. He almost sounded disappointed. Fortune went to twine around his boots as if offering solace.

Elspeth glanced around. "But can nothing be done

to punish Lord Westerbrook? He may not have robbed anyone, but he instigated the attacks."

"If he truly is having financial difficulties, his creditors will hound him," Mr. Keller offered.

"And Lord Norfall may have something to say in the matter," Meredith put in as Roth resumed his seat. "We might have difficulty holding a peer to account, but he will not. I'll write to him this very afternoon."

As the conversation continued, Fortune abandoned Mr. Roth and came to jump up into Julia's lap. She snuggled deep into the folds of the wool gown. Julia ran a hand down the soft, grey fur.

"You knew, didn't you?" she murmured. "You never liked Lord Westerbrook."

In response, Fortune shuddered and sneezed.

Julia laughed. Another match to the cat's credit, and the perfect man for her. She had found her way to Tanner, and she would never let him go.

The adventure was just beginning.

Meredith sat on the sofa in the withdrawing room the next day, hand running idly down Fortune's fur. She should be so pleased. Roth's employer was delighted with him and had recently given him a raise in pay. Finn was happily married to Abigail, and both were doing fine work according to the letter that had come from Ivy, the Marchioness of Kendall, who, with her husband, were their new patrons.

Tanner and Julia had seemed so happy yesterday. She looked forward to hearing about all the places they would go and all the things they would do together. She had not thought to see Keller engaged to one of the Bees, but she had to own Elspeth was an unexpected dear, and if anyone could turn her mother up sweet, it would be the good-natured Keller.

It seemed her work was done.

And yet…

Roth didn't look as happy about his future as his employer did. He had ever been the most pessimistic of the quartet. Now he seemed resigned. She would have to give the matter some thought. How lovely it would be to enjoy Christmas, knowing her four guards were well settled, especially as Julian had written that the agreement had been ratified, and he would be coming home.

"I'll make every effort to reach you by Christmas, darling," he'd said. "We can host the annual Christmas Eve party together. We have much to celebrate."

Fortune raised her head a moment before the knocker sounded below. She slipped off Meredith's lap and padded to the landing to peer through the balusters. A few moments later, and she was ushering Cowls into the room.

"Lady Alldene is here, your ladyship. Are you at home?"

Interesting. "Certainly, Cowls. Is it just the countess or her children as well?" She hadn't had an opportunity to prepare Fortune for the threesome.

"The countess appears to be alone, your ladyship," he replied.

"Then please show her up."

He did just that. As at the railway demonstration, Lady Alldene was gowned in black, from the net veil to the black half-boots peeking out from under her unadorned black lustring gown. She peeled off the veil to reveal sleeked-back platinum hair and offered Meredith a tentative smile.

"How very nice to see you, Countess," Meredith said, indicating the closest chair. "To what do I owe the pleasure?"

She sank onto the chair, graceful hands pressing together in her lap. "I understood from Mr. Tanner's note that he and Miss Hewett will be married."

"Indeed," Meredith said. "Very happy news for all concerned."

"It most certainly is. But we had spoken about the possibility of one of your guards coming to work for me."

"So we had," Meredith agreed. "A tutor, you said?"

"Yes. As I mentioned, my husband's will names his cousin, Westerbrook, the guardian for my sons. You can understand why I might find that arrangement less than satisfactory."

She could indeed, given all Julia had recently told her of the fellow. Lady Alldene had obviously seen his lordship's dark side and had tried to warn Julia about it.

"He has a different opinion on how your sons should be raised?" Meredith asked.

She lifted her nose. "He insists that I am not sufficiently stern with them. If I disagree with him on any particular, he threatens to remove them to a school where they might better learn to be gentlemen."

"My Julian met many of his friends at such a school," Meredith pointed out. "It seems to be expected."

Her pretty face tightened. "Many young men attend such schools, but if Westerbrook is an example of what those schools produce, my sons would do better to remain with me." She edged forward on her seat. "I thought if I had a fearsome tutor for the boys, that might give him pause and offer me a chance of fighting him in Chancelry Court should he decide to make good on his threats."

Meredith studied her. Her blue eyes sparkled with intelligence and a degree of hope, but it would be difficult for any mother to meet the standards of education expected of a peer of the realm. A guard might indeed impart wisdom to her sons and help her protect them. But if Norfall could not or would not bring a case against Lord Westerbrook in the House of Lords, the viscount could be particularly difficult about having another Imperial Guard involved. After all, Tanner had ousted him from Julia's affections. The countess could be making things worse for herself.

As if she saw Meredith's hesitation, Lady Alldene's serene face crumbled. "Please, Lady Belfort. I have loved only four people in my life, and one has been taken from me. I cannot allow Westerbrook to take two more."

Fortune came from behind the sofa and prowled up to the countess to lay a paw on her gown as if offering a blessing. Another lady might have pulled the fine material away or even nudged Fortune with her boot. Lady Alldene merely gazed down and mouthed, "Thank you."

Meredith raised her head. "Three of my four guards have found suitable positions, but Mr. Roth, who has been their leader, may be looking for something better. He and I will come see you at first convenience."

She sagged. "Thank you, Lady Belfort. You cannot know how you have eased my mind."

"Glad to help, my dear. After all, every family needs its own hero."

THANKS FOR READING Tanner and Julia's story. They were two adventurous souls who discovered it was sweeter to rely on each other. If you missed any of the Fortune's Brides stories, you can find them all on my website at www.reginascott.com.

Stephen Roth may have something to say to the dastardly Westerbrook, if he can learn from the countess what it means to join a family. Turn the page for a sneak peek of *Never Hire a Hero*.

SNEAK PEEK

BOOK
THREE
Guarding Her Heart

REGINA SCOTT

CHAPTER ONE

Near Alldene Castle, Surrey
Early December 1825

OF ALL THE enemies he'd faced over the years, he'd never thought two boys would be the most daunting.

Stephen Roth leaned back against the squabs of the coach that was trundling west toward Alldene Castle, the site of his new assignment. The winter landscape seemed as bleak as his thoughts. His fingers fisted in his lap.

"You are exactly what the countess needs," Lady Belfort said across from him.

She, at least, seemed to have no misgivings. Roth appreciated that about her. From the swan's down edging her quilted winter cloak to the embroidered wool skirts peeking out below, his patroness was the epitome of good taste and propriety. Her hair was as dark as his, her eyes a remarkable shade of lavender to his sword-edge grey. She must have been enamored by the color, for her gowns and coats inevitably matched it.

"I will endeavor to bring only praise to your efforts, your ladyship," he said.

She cocked her head. "Why, Mr. Roth, if I didn't know better, I might think you were nervous."

She didn't know the half of it. He had served his king and princes for most of his life, but they had elected to either return to their home country, Batavaria, or start new lives here in England. He could not return to Batavaria, and so far, his life in England had been less than what he'd hoped.

An Imperial Guard, a member of that elite force, renowned across the Continent for bravery, skills, honor, reduced to guarding a steam manufactory at night.

And now, a tutor.

A movement across the coach drew his eye. Lady Belfort's cat, Fortune, arched her back and stretched before affixing him with her copper-colored gaze. Roth did not so much as smile, but he wiggled a finger against his trousers.

The cat lowered her head and raised her haunches, watching.

"You are teasing her," Lady Belfort said with a smile.

"I never tease," Roth said. He wiggled his fingers again, and the cat leaped across the coach to pounce on him. He raised both hands. "I surrender."

As if well pleased with herself, Fortune began rubbing against his thigh.

"We will need to keep a close eye on her at the castle," Lady Belfort said. "I understand there are far too many places to hide." She nodded out the window. "You can see it now."

Hand running down the cat's grey fur, he glanced out the window. On a hill overlooking a narrow valley split by a winding stream, Alldene Castle glowed like gold in the light of the winter sun. A square tower guarded each of the front corners, with a wider gatehouse in the middle. A bailey with a crenelated top led from one to the other. It was shorter than the Great Keep of Batavaria, and stouter than the castle they had stayed in in the German states. Still, he could appreciate the fortifications. If they had their own water supply, they could hold out against a siege for months.

Not that anyone would lay siege to them in Surrey. Worse luck.

The closer they came, however, the more he frowned. Were those pitched rooftops right up against the bailey? A well-placed arrow could light the whole place on fire. And the windows on the ground floor were far too wide to allow for protection.

But he had to own it was nice to hear the drawbridge rattle as the coach crossed it.

"They still have a moat," he said.

"I imagine you're one of the few to appreciate that fact," Lady Belfort replied as the coach drew to a stop in the cobbled inner courtyard.

He had been right about the house. Shaped like a U, it filled the inside, from stone wall to stone wall. It was half timbered, the panels scrubbed white between the thick, tarred oak beams, and the windows consisted of dozens of tiny panes of glass shaped like diamonds.

"Built in the sixteenth century," Lady Belfort commented. "But modernized since, I have heard."

That would account for the larger windows on the outside. Modernization was all well and good, so long as it kept the family safe.

A tall fellow with pomaded hair the same color as the castle walls and the regal bearing of a butler appeared from the doorway along the back of the courtyard as a footman jogged forward to open the door. Roth jumped down, then handed Lady Belfort to the grey stones of the courtyard, Fortune secured in her arms.

"Lady Belfort, Mr. Roth," the butler said with a bow. "Welcome to Alldene. Her ladyship is expecting you. If you'd be so kind." He waved toward the doorway.

The entire time, he smiled. As if having them there was such an honor he could not help but puff out his chest. Perhaps it was Lady Belfort who had impressed him.

Roth followed her and the butler into a dimly lit

corridor that stretched in either direction, then accepted Fortune from her so another footman could take her cloak. The cat wiggled against his coat, but he kept his hold gentle. He wasn't entirely certain why Lady Belfort had decided to bring her pet, but he would do nothing that might endanger Fortune. She was a legend, having matched a dozen well-placed lords over the years, including his own prince, Otto Leopold.

As he waited, he glanced around. After what he'd seen outside, he could only conclude that the occupants of Alldene Castle had trouble making up their minds about their home. The two-story entry hall just ahead was paneled at the bottom with dark wood, while a gallery of the same wood loomed over the left side. Along with the stone hearth and suit of armor in one corner, it should have been a brooding, masculine place. But every bit of the wood was elaborately carved in flowers, and the burning fire could only be called cheery.

As Roth handed Fortune back to his patroness, the butler led them down the left corridor and around another corner. The southwest quadrant of the castle, then. The fellow opened a paneled door to let them into a long withdrawing room. Again, the walls were covered with the dark paneling, highly polished here, and it covered the hearth as well, but the expanse of carpet showed medallions of roses, and all the furniture was dainty and elegant and done in shades of pink or cream.

That elegance was nothing to the lady who stood at the sight of them. He'd seen Lady Alldene when he'd been helping his friend, Tanner, guard a railway opening last month. She was tall, willowy, and always draped in black. Today, the net veil flowed from her carefully coiffed pale blond hair to the hem of her simple black gown.

"Lady Belfort, Mr. Roth," she heralded. "Thank you so much for coming."

Lady Belfort went to sit beside her on one of the

velvet-upholstered sofas. Roth started toward the wall, to take up his usual spot, before realizing he didn't need to guard those in the room. He wasn't here to protect the countess, just her sons.

Even if something inside him urged him to protect her.

Habit. She might appear as if a good wind would bowl her over, but she likely needed no protection here in her great castle with her doting staff. Even now the butler was adding more coal to the fire as if to ensure her comfort.

He took a chair not too far away from the ladies and rested his palms on his knees.

Lady Belfort released Fortune, who slipped away from her to crawl into the countess's lap. Some of the tension in his shoulders eased. It was said that if Fortune approved of you, you were of very fine character indeed. He should not wonder that she appreciated the lovely countess.

He still remained astonished that she approved of him.

"I see you brought a friend," Lady Alldene said. Her long-fingered hand was gentle on the silky coat.

"I always take Fortune with me, so long as it is safe for her," Lady Belfort confessed. "She has a great gift for understanding people, far more than I will ever possess. She is very fond of Mr. Roth."

As if she knew her cue, Fortune jumped down onto the flowered carpet and padded toward him. She wound her way around his boots, purr audible against the crack of the fire.

"I will own to finding that comforting," Lady Alldene said with a look in his direction.

He stopped himself from bending to stroke the cat. Comforting? Had she had doubts about him?

What had she heard? Who had told her about his past?

"Indeed," Lady Belfort said with a nod to him. She turned her gaze on the countess once more. "You can understand why I am protective of my guards. I agreed to find them suitable positions here in England. Mr. Roth has not been appropriately appreciated so far."

He hadn't realized she knew he was unhappy. He had tried his best to do whatever work was given him. Anything was better than returning to Batavaria.

"Well, we will do our best to appreciate his talents here," Lady Alldene said. "Felden, would you make sure Mr. Roth's things are taken up to the tutor's room?"

"Of course, your ladyship," her butler assured her.

Lady Belfort held up a hand as if to stop him. "First, I have a few questions of my own. I understand you are engaging him as a tutor to your two sons, Lord Shaw and James."

Lady Alldene inclined her head. "That is correct. I have a nurse for Lady Audra, my daughter."

That was to the good. He was never sure what to do with little girls. They seemed so… breakable.

"And you wish him to school them in all the gentlemanly arts," Lady Belfort persisted.

"Reading, mathematics, geography, the sciences," Lady Alldene rattled off, each word a stone dropping into his stomach. Would she sack him immediately if she knew he had studied those things for only two years before joining the military?

"And of course riding, fencing, archery, and fisticuffs."

He blew out a breath. Those he could do. Those he excelled at.

"Very good," Lady Belfort said. "He will need a half day off each week, the opportunity to attend services on Sundays and holy days, and his own room as well as board."

"Certainly," the countess said. "And a mount at his disposal."

That could be a boon. He might ride out once the weather was warmer, see something outside the castle walls.

Which oddly felt as if they were growing closer.

"Then we are agreed," Lady Belfort said as if she'd finished negotiating the price for a new length of lace. "Only one thing remains. I would like to have Fortune meet your children."

From the moment Thea had first met the cat, she could tell that Lady Belfort and Fortune shared a great bond. Still, she hadn't expected her new friend to bring the creature with her to Alldene, and she certainly hadn't expected her to want to introduce Fortune to the children.

It was going to be difficult enough introducing them to her sons' new tutor.

She couldn't help glancing at the fellow again. Did that chiseled face ever smile? She'd wanted someone sufficiently stern to cow her nemesis, Lord Westerbrook. But those steely grey eyes could likely give at least James, her youngest son, nightmares.

Perhaps she had made a mistake.

No! That fear has raised its head far too many times since Thomas had died. She was Lady Alldene, a countess in her own right. She had been born in this castle, she had grown up in this castle, and she had been trained to rule this castle and all the lands surrounding it. She didn't need anyone.

Most of the time.

"Felden," she said to her butler. "Would you be so kind as to ask Nurse Waters to bring the children down?"

"At once, your ladyship."

At least Felden never argued with her. He had been head footman when the butler she'd known growing up had retired and had been a logical choice to promote, Thomas had said. She'd agreed. Felden was organized, polished, and efficient, with a surprisingly affable nature for a butler. She could not ask for more.

But what should she ask of this man?

He was watching her now, eyes narrowing, as if he saw the doubts flickering inside her like a guttering candle. She raised her chin and met him look for look. She might wonder over tenant questions and tithes, but she was unwavering in one area.

The protection and happiness of her children. If hiring this man could keep them by her side, she would be willing to give him anything.

Lady Belfort rose and went to collect her pet, who was still strolling back and forth around Mr. Roth's boots as if polishing them to ensure he would look tip-top for the coming introduction. She was a lovely creature, with silvery grey fur and white around her throat like a cravat. She gazed at Thea with eyes the color of copper kettles, tail swinging idly back and forth, as her mistress resumed her seat.

"I do hope you and your family will join us for our Christmas Eve party," Lady Belfort said. "We have held it every year since I was a girl. The pond generally ices up, so there should be skating. And if this weather holds, we might even have snow for sleigh rides and snowball fights."

At the last word, his lips twitched. Yes, she would imagine fights of any kind would amuse him.

"That sounds lovely," Thea said, focusing on her friend. "I'm sure the children would enjoy it."

As if in answer, Nurse Waters trotted into the room, one hand holding Audra's. Waters was ample in every aspect, both in her well-rounded appearance and in the attentions she lavished on her charges. Ten-year-old Shaw stood on one side, nose up and gaze watchful. Eight-year-old James, on her other side, was glancing around as if trying to determine what he might have done to be required so suddenly. Both favored her more than Thomas, though their hair was closer to brown than blond, their eyes a darker shade of blue.

"Children," Thea said, beckoning them closer. "You remember Lady Belfort from the railway demonstration last month. You may also remember Mr. Roth."

Audra brightened until she looked so much like dark-haired Thomas that Thea's heart clenched. "You fought off those bad robbers."

"There are no good robbers, silly," Shaw pointed out with a shake of his head.

Audra's smile popped, and she glared at her brother.

"Mr. Roth was indeed a hero that day," Thea said, pulling their attention back to her. "That is why I suggested to Lady Belfort that we might hire him as your tutor, boys."

James' brows shot up. Shaw crossed his arms over his chest. But before he could start the rebellion she could see simmering in his eyes, Audra pulled out of the nurse's grip.

"Can't he be my tutor too?" she begged. "I want a tutor, Mother."

"Girls don't have tutors," Shaw said. "They have governesses. And you're too little for one anyway."

She stomped her foot. "Am not!"

"Are so," Shaw countered.

"He's probably right," James hazarded.

"Children!" Thea rose, face hot. Thomas had always known what to say, what to do, to bring out the best in them. Was she such an unnatural mother that she couldn't do the same?

Lady Belfort opened her arms and allowed her pet to drop to the carpet.

Once more, Audra's face lit. "Kitty!"

Fortune shook herself as if shuddering.

"She isn't too fond of that word," Lady Belfort said with a smile. "Her name is Fortune, and she would like to make your acquaintance."

Waters took a step forward, round face pinching. "Your ladyship, I must protest. Cats are filthy things, better suited to barns and such."

Lady Belfort stiffened. "I can assure you, madam, that Fortune is bathed regularly and brushed twice daily. She is no more filthy than you are after a day of chasing children about."

The nurse puffed herself up.

"That will be all, Waters," Thea said, and the woman swirled and marched out.

In the meantime, Fortune had prowled closer to her daughter. Audra dropped to the carpet in a pool of muslin and held out a hand. "Nice cat. Lovely cat. Would you like to be friends?"

Shaw snorted. "Cats aren't friends."

"She looks friendly." James knelt beside his sister, who was petting the cat with such gentleness that Thea's heart swelled.

"If you don't need me, Mother," Shaw said, "I was in the middle of plotting strategy."

Her oldest son and heir might pretend to great sophistication, but she knew that strategy he was devising had to do with the hundred lead soldiers who were endlessly battling across his room. At least he hadn't started to behave with the condescension of Lord Westerbrook yet. What he really needed was a father, but she wasn't ready to give him one. She might never be ready to give him one again.

Fortune had pulled away from Audra to suffer James' touch. A smile curved her youngest son's lips, one of the first she'd seen in a long time. Again, her heart twinged.

Then the cat approached Shaw.

Shaw looked down his nose at her.

Fortune sat, gazing up at him, head cocked, as if considering.

Thea thought she wasn't the only one holding her breath.

Fortune turned and went back to Audra and James.

Shaw sagged as if he knew he had somehow failed.

Thea glanced to Lady Belfort, who rose. "Two out of three isn't bad. I'm sure we can improve the odds in the future. I believe Mr. Roth can stay."

Shaw's head came back up. "So, we're to have Mr. Roth as our tutor, are we? I should think I would have a say in the matter."

The challenge was entirely too clear. Thomas would have known how to defuse the situation. She was highly tempted to send her son to his room until he apologized.

But she was interested in seeing how this man would take such a challenge.

She turned to Mr. Roth. "Well, sir? What do you think?"

Learn more at www.reginascott.com/hero.html.

OTHER BOOKS BY REGINA SCOTT

Fortune's Brides Series

Never Doubt a Duke
Never Borrow a Baronet
Never Envy an Earl
Never Vie for a Viscount
Never Kneel to a Knight
Never Marry a Marquess
Always Kiss at Christmas
Never Pursue a Prince
Never Court a Count
Never Romance a Rogue
Never Love a Lord
Never Beguile a Bodyguard

Grace-by-the-Sea Series

The Matchmaker's Rogue
The Heiress's Convenient Husband
The Artist's Healer
The Governess's Earl
The Lady's Second-Chance Suitor
The Siren's Captain

Uncommon Courtships Series

The Unflappable Miss Fairchild
The Incomparable Miss Compton
The Irredeemable Miss Renfield
The Unwilling Miss Watkin
An Uncommon Christmas

Lady Emily Capers

Secrets and Sensibilities
Art and Artifice
Ballrooms and Blackmail
Eloquence and Espionage
Love and Larceny

Marvelous Munroes Series

My True Love Gave to Me
The Rogue Next Door
The Marquis' Kiss
A Match for Mother

Spy Matchmaker Series

The Husband Mission
The June Bride Conspiracy
The Heiress Objective

The Regent's Devices Trilogy (writing as R.E. Scott with Shelley Adina)

The Emperor's Aeronaut
The Prince's Pilot
The Lady's Triumph

Frontier Matches

The Perfect Mail-Order Bride
Her Frontier Sweethearts
Frontier Cinderella

And other books from
Harper Collins, Mirror Press, and Revell.

ABOUT THE AUTHOR

REGINA SCOTT STARTED writing novels in the third grade. Thankfully for literature as we know it, she didn't sell her first novel until she learned a bit more about writing. Since her first book was published, her stories have traveled the globe, with translations in many languages including Dutch, German, Italian, and Portuguese. She now has more than 65 published works of warm, witty romance, and more than one million copies of her books are in reader hands.

Alas, she cannot have a cat of her own, as her husband is allergic to them. Fortune the cat belongs to her critique partner and dear friend Kristy J. Manhattan, who supports pet rescue groups and spoils her four-footed family members. If Fortune resembles any cat you know, credit Kristy.

Regina Scott and her husband of more than 30 years reside in the Puget Sound area of Washington State. She has dressed as a Regency dandy, driven four-in-hand, learned to fence, and sailed on a tall ship, all in the name of research, of course. Learn more about her at her website at *www.reginascott.com*.